Vocations

Heather Beck

Syren Books

Vocations
Copyright © 2013 Heather Beck
Cover Photo Copyright © J. Plus/Fotolia

Published by
Syren Books

Library and Archives Canada Cataloguing in Publication

Beck, Heather, 1985-
Vocations / Heather Beck.

Issued also in an electronic format.
ISBN 978-1-926990-12-5

I. Title.

PS8603.E423V62 2013 jC813'.6 C2012-907771-2

Table of Contents:

Part One:

♡

The Vocation Test

It was a cold mid-afternoon in January as snow fell upon the American city of Cascade. The sky was cloudy and dark, telltale signs that a storm was brewing. Nestled amongst this threatening atmosphere was Western Heights High School. Built just a decade ago, the institution had quickly gained recognition for its academically-inclined programs. Today, an unexpected message interrupted the classes at Western Heights.

"Will all teachers of the senior level please immediately guide their class to the auditorium? That's all senior classes to the auditorium. Thank you." A loud click echoed afterwards, indicating that the principal, Mr. Russell, had switched off the PA system.

"I wonder what the assembly is about," Jeannie whispered to Lila and Pamela as their teacher, Mrs. Davenport, led the students to the auditorium.

"It's probably an award ceremony to honor my latest article in the school newspaper," Pamela said dreamily.

Ever since Pamela's article on the school's dress code was published on the front page of Western Heights News, it was all she could think about.

"I'm sure that's the reason," Jeannie replied, rolling her eyes.

As the three friends walked down the hall and chatted quietly, they looked like they had been best friends forever. Those who made this presumption were absolutely right.

Each girl looked very different from the other. Short and a little overweight, Pamela Mitchell had medium length brown curly hair and sparkling blue eyes. She could usually be seen wearing an indie rock band t-shirt and a comfortable pair of jeans. Being a strong follower of social liberalism, she strived to change the world a little at a time through her non-fiction writing.

Lila Ford wasn't as concerned about world issues as Pamela. She preferred to spend her free time taking pictures of landscapes and animals. Lila was an avid outdoorswoman who claimed she was happiest when surrounded by wilderness with nothing but a camera in her hands and friends by her side. Lila was constantly being told how pretty she was – a comment which annoyed her fiercely. She said it was pointless for a photographer to be beautiful since photographers only cared about what was in front of the lens. Lila stood tall at five foot eight; she was well-built from all the exercise she got while searching for potential photographic images in the woods. However, it was Lila's long red hair and piercing green eyes which were her best features.

Jeannie Dallas was in between Pamela and Lila's height. She had short blonde hair, hazel eyes and a dimple in her right cheek that appeared every time she smiled. Unlike Pamela and Lila, she didn't have a passion that she pursued whole-heartedly. Jeannie liked most things and didn't believe that one must have an innate desire for something to be happy.

Since Pamela, Lila and Jeannie seemed so different, many of their classmates wondered why they shared such a strong bond. Their friendship was based upon a sincere liking for each other and the history they shared.

During their first days at Western Heights Elementary, Pamela, Lila and Jeannie met under unusual circumstances. The school outing to a local amusement park led them to a rollercoaster which promised to be the fastest, scariest and wildest ride they'd ever been on. Fate, as Pamela liked to define it, made them line up one after the other and brought them to sit in the same rollercoaster compartment. It was in the spinning, diving and jerky rollercoaster where Jeannie threw up and, in a subsequent action, Pamela and Lila bumped heads. After their classmates heard about the mortifying incident, they were subjected to social mockery for a week. In that isolated week, Pamela, Lila and Jeannie turned to each other for support and friendship. They found this in one another and held on to it ever since.

With only a quarter of the auditorium's seats occupied, Mrs. Davenport's class filed in. Pamela, Lila and Jeannie had no trouble finding seats together as Mr. Russell began to talk.

"I'm sure you are all curious as to why you're here. I have gathered all the seniors together to discuss a very important matter. This matter relates to the process of applying to colleges and universities. I don't mean to sound condescending, but for those of you who haven't noticed, we are already halfway into the school year. It's time that you began to think about where you'd like to go next fall. I was once a student myself, so I understand the confusion and panic some of you may be feeling. To help ease these unnecessary emotions, our dedicated guidance counselors have created a vocation test."

"Did he just say we're going to do a vacation test?" Jeannie asked in confusion. "What in the world is a vacation test?"

"Not a vacation test," Pamela replied. "He said a *vocation* test. It's a quiz that determines what we're good at. It tells us what career path we should take."

Lila snorted loudly, causing Pamela and Jeannie to turn their attention towards her. "Mr. Russell must be joking," she commented with a hint of snootiness. "I already know what I want to be. I'd never let a piece of paper tell me differently."

"I agree with you," Pamela added. "Tests like these place people into stereotypical groups based on a few inane questions. It's like peer pressure but even worse since many people foolishly believe those in authority know something they don't. Tests like these can be blamed for lack of personal achievement and the inevitable onset of depression. The government and school systems say vocational tests better our society by inspiring students to gain employment. That reasoning is just plain wrong. It kills all creativity!"

"Okay, Pamela," a wide-eyed Jeannie urged. "We get your point. Now would you mind turning the volume on your mouth down? People are starting to stare." Jeannie didn't really care that people were looking at them. She was used to it since Pamela usually had a political or social opinion outburst every week. She was annoyed, however, at Pamela and Lila's insensitivity. Jeannie was unsure about her future career plans. She thought they could at least consider that she might be interested in taking the vocation test.

After receiving a box containing several vocation tests, the teachers and their students went back to their classrooms. When everyone was seated once again, Mrs. Davenport began handing out the tests.

"No, thank you," Pamela said as Mrs. Davenport approached her with the test. "I've already chosen my career."

Mrs. Davenport ignored Pamela's protest as she tossed a test on her desk.

"A lack of substantial education *and* a test that belittles individuality," Pamela whispered to Jeannie and Lila. "What's the world coming to?"

Jeannie ignored her friend's words as she began reading the vocation test.

Question number one: You just arrived at the mall with your friends. They agree to let you pick the first store to visit. You choose:

A) A clothing store

B) A pet store

C) A music or game store

D) A craft store

E) A book store

Jeannie bit her lip while she concentrated on the question. She finally chose answer A.

Question number two: When an event occurs in your life that makes you mad, you:

A) Go shopping or concentrate on an upcoming event by planning what you will wear

B) Focus on other people's problems and try to help them. You know that thinking about yourself all the time isn't good for your mental health

C) Close your bedroom door and turn up the music or play a video game. Within a few minutes of engaging in the chosen activity, you have completely forgotten about your problem

D) Make something. Make anything. If you're not literally building something now, you're planning for it. You'll do anything creative because it helps to take your mind off the unpleasant event

E) Read. There is no better way to escape reality than through a good book

Answer B suited Jeannie.

Question number three: You would describe yourself as:

A) Being a sociable person

B) Someone who is very sympathetic and caring towards others

C) Someone who likes to create new things from existing technology

D) Someone who likes to think outside the box

E) An intellectual who loves to expand his/her knowledge

The best answer was B, again, in Jeannie's opinion.

Question number four: You must pick one more course to complete your timetable. You choose:

A) A social science course

B) Biology

C) Music

D) Workshop

E) A course on literature

A, definitely A, she decided.

Question number five: If a friend has a problem, they would count on you to:

A) Offer insight which he/she may have overlooked

B) Be a shoulder to cry on

C) Allow him/her to forget about the problem by engaging in a fun activity requiring a lot of concentration

D) Help him/her figure out a detailed plan to fix the problem

E) Compare the situation to a problem faced by a literary character and then suggest he/she do what the character did

Another B, Jeannie thought while circling her answer. She anxiously flipped to the last page where a description of the answers was offered.

If you chose mainly A's, you are very people-oriented. You would be good at the following jobs: social worker, retail, fashion consultant, secretary.

If you chose mainly B's, you express an interest in, and understanding of, the sciences. You would be good at the following jobs: veterinarian, doctor, dentist.

If you chose mainly C's, you are creative in various forms of media. You would be good at the following jobs: arts management, musician, video game designer/tester.

If you chose mainly D's, you often have unique ideas. You would be good at the following jobs: entrepreneur, manager.

If you chose mainly E's, you love the written word. You would be good at the following jobs: author, editor, English teacher, journalist, librarian.

Jeannie had picked mainly B's and was extremely upset by the vocation test's outcome. She hadn't taken any high school courses to prepare for such careers. Positive that she didn't want to spend her whole life studying, Jeannie tossed the vocation test into her backpack.

A bell rang, signaling the end of the school day. Chairs scraped noisily against the hard floor as the students hurried to leave.

"You look upset, Jeannie," Lila noted as she slipped her blue and green backpack over her shoulder. "Is everything alright?"

"I guess so," Jeannie replied unhappily.

"You don't look fine," Pamela pointed out as they walked down the hall and towards their lockers.

"I am a little upset," Jeannie confessed as she opened her locker and pulled out her jacket. "I know you both think vocation tests are stupid, but I'm really confused about what I'll do next year. I feel like I have to make a decision soon."

Pamela bit her tongue. She desperately wanted to point out how self-destructive vocation tests could be. Instead, Pamela offered Jeannie a comforting smile. "A lot of people don't know what they want to do."

"You two do," Jeannie said bitterly while shutting her locker.

"I just discovered my love for photography three years ago," Lila stated. "You'll find your true passion one day soon."

The three friends continued walking down the hall while talking about their plans for that night.

Lila said she was going to the mall to buy a digital photo frame.

Pamela told Lila and Jeannie she was going to compile her latest research and form it into an article.

"Jeannie," Pamela inquired when her friend failed to speak. "Earth to Jeannie."

"What is it?" Jeannie finally asked.

"I would know that look anywhere," Lila said with a laugh. "It's the I'm in love with Doug Kenningson daze."

Jeannie watched as the tall boy with brown hair and blue eyes cast a glance in her direction before continuing down the hall.

"Did you see that?" Jeannie whispered with heightening excitement. "Doug checked me out!"

"Sure he did," Pamela said with a playful laugh.

"He did," Jeannie insisted angrily.

"I wasn't looking – sorry," Lila added.

Pamela suddenly realized Doug was a touchy topic for her smitten friend. "I'm just kidding," she said apologetically.

"Doug definitely looked in my direction," Jeannie continued to argue.

"I believe you," Pamela said, raising her hands in defeat. "I wasn't looking at him either, so what would I know?"

"How can you guys not look at Doug?" Jeannie gushed. "He has the body of a professional athlete. I've also heard he has a heart of gold. Did you guys know that Doug donated the most items for the Children's Hospital toy drive? He's just so wonderful!"

"I'm not into the athletic type," Pamela said. "They're too clichéd."

"Surely Lila agrees with me, right?" Jeannie asked hopefully.

"There's nothing wrong with Doug," Lila admitted. "And I do like his charitable nature."

"See, I'm not the only one who thinks Doug Kenningson is hot!"

"I didn't say that," Lila objected, a bit embarrassed by Jeannie's loud tone of voice.

"Whatever, Lila," Jeannie said with a giggle. "You better not steal him away from me though!"

"There's no chance of that happening," Lila replied truthfully. "I'm far too concerned with my photography right now."

Jeannie felt her smile fade. Lila's mention of photography made her think about her own career, or more specifically, her lack of one.

"Jeannie, why aren't you eating your dinner?" Mrs. Dallas inquired later that night.

Startled by her mother's voice, Jeannie looked up. "What did you just say?"

"I asked why you aren't eating your dinner. Do you feel alright?"

Jeannie sighed. She was getting sick of people asking about her health. "I feel fine," she lied.

"I understand your lack of enthusiasm towards the broccoli, but why haven't you touched the macaroni and cheese? It's your favorite meal."

Jeannie was so wrapped up in her thoughts that she had forgotten to eat. She dug her fork into the macaroni and cheese and pulled out a big clump. She stuffed it into her mouth and chewed.

"See, I'm eating," she said in between mouthfuls.

"Jeannie Ann Dallas," Mrs. Dallas said in a stern voice, "Tell me what is on your mind right now. You and I have to be straight with each other. If something's bothering you, I should know about it."

Jeannie knew her mother was only trying to help. However, her method wasn't as helpful as it used to be. Jeannie couldn't blame her though. After her father's death, her mom didn't have time to coax Jeannie's problems out of her slowly. Jeannie could see that being a single mom with a full-time job didn't leave room for much else.

"I do have something on my mind," Jeannie finally said. "It's about college."

Her mother suddenly looked sullen. She nodded, encouraging Jeannie to continue speaking.

"We took a vocation test in school today. I know they're silly, but the careers the test said I would be good at didn't interest me at all. It said I should be a veterinarian, a doctor or a dentist. How crazy is that?"

"I don't think it's crazy," Mrs. Dallas replied. "You're a very smart girl."

10

"I'm average," Jeannie corrected her quickly.

"You could be a veterinarian, a doctor or a dentist if you wanted." Mrs. Dallas let out a soft sigh. "You *are* smart enough, but I don't know where the money for all those years of education would come from."

Jeannie felt her face go red with embarrassment as she watched her mother force back the tears that threatened to slide down her face at any second. Jeannie knew that now was the right time to tell her mother what she had decided earlier.

"Mom," Jeannie said softly. "I don't want to go to college."

Mrs. Dallas looked at her daughter in surprise. "You're just saying that because of our money situation. You can get a school loan or I can get one from the bank. Either way, you *are* going to college."

"Mom, I really don't want to go – at least not yet," Jeannie said forcefully. "My decision is based upon my uncertainty of what I want to do as a career. It has very little to do with money."

Mrs. Dallas looked closely at Jeannie as if she could gain the truth by peering into her soul. "Do you really want to postpone college?" she finally asked.

"Yes," Jeannie answered assertively. "I'm going to start searching for a job right away. I'll work part-time for now and then full-time after school finishes in the spring. I'll work until I figure out what I want to do with my life."

"You sound like you know what you're doing," her mother commented.

"I do, sort of."

"Then it's fine by me. Remember that college will always be there. Don't give up your education just because you're unsure of what to study."

11

"I won't," Jeannie replied as she got up from her seat and hurried over to her mother. Jeannie wrapped her arms around her and squeezed gently. "I love you, Mom."

"I love you too. Now eat your dinner before it gets cold."

* * *

Sitting in her bedroom, Jeannie stared at the open history book lying on her desk. She was in the middle of reading about the Civil War, but she couldn't concentrate on the words. It was a sunny Saturday afternoon in late April, and all she could think about was the fact that she hadn't had a single job interview even though she'd submitted her resume to numerous stores. The lack of interviews was annoying her more than ever, and Pamela and Lila were to be blamed for her anxious feelings. They were super busy preparing their entrance portfolios for the specialized programs in journalism and photography. Jeannie felt Pamela and Lila were advancing in life, while she did nothing but strive for a high school diploma. Still satisfied with her decision to postpone college, she just wished she could get a job to support her decision.

Ring. Ring. Ring.

"Hello?" Jeannie greeted, after reaching for the telephone.

"Hi, Jeannie," Lila said excitedly. "I just got back from the post office. I mailed my portfolio to the university!"

"That's great," Jeannie replied with a mixture of sincerity and jealousy.

"Yeah, I'm glad it's finished. I've been so nervous about it since I received the application form and details of the entrance project."

"That's to be expected," Jeannie reassured Lila. "I talked to Pamela earlier today and she said she's finally chosen which articles to include in her entrance submission."

"It took her long enough," Lila said through a giggle. "Have you received any calls from employers?" she asked, growing serious.

Jeannie felt her cheeks burn with embarrassment. She felt uncomfortable talking about her lack of employment, especially after Lila had discussed her latest step towards an amazing career.

"No," Jeannie answered in a nonchalant tone.

"Then you can apply for a job at my uncle's restaurant," Lila offered. "One of his employees just got married and moved to a new state. Uncle Michael is looking for a full-time waitress. Are you interested?"

"Yes!" Jeannie answered enthusiastically. She had visited Michael's restaurant several times, and she thought it was a beautiful place with excellent food.

"You'll have an advantage over the other candidates. I already told him what a hard worker you are."

"I really appreciate the referral," Jeannie said sincerely.

"At the risk of sounding clichéd," Lila began with a chuckle, "what are friends for?"

After Jeannie said goodbye to Lila, she dialed the phone number she'd just been given. As the phone rang, she felt a mixture of excitement and nervousness.

A man with a deep voice answered. "Hello?"

"Hello, my name is Jeannie Dallas. I'm a friend of the Ford's. I'm looking for a job and they mentioned you needed a waitress."

"Jeannie Dallas!" Michael replied in a loud, friendly voice. "I remember Lila bringing you and another friend to my restaurant. Tell me, are you the blonde or the brunette?"

"Blonde."

"Oh yes, I remember you perfectly. There's no need to be so formal with me, Jeannie. How have you been keeping?"

"I've been very well, thank you, and yourself?"

"Extremely busy. You were right to say I need a waitress. My last waiter left me with hardly a week's notice. He moved to Arizona to get hitched. I'm really swamped."

"I'm sorry to hear that. I'm sure I would be able to help you though. I'm able to work weekday nights and weekends. And you'll be happy to know that my schedule will be completely free from July onward."

"Yes, Lila told me all about you. I was hoping you'd call. I'll happily offer you the waitress position, but before you give me an answer, I want to tell you what the job entails. It's a standard waitress job. Have you ever worked in the service sector before?"

"No, but I'm a fast learner."

"That's okay, honey. No experience is necessary. We all have to start somewhere, after all. You'll be expected to take the customer's orders and serve the meal to them. The pay is minimum, plus any tips received."

"The job sounds great," Jeannie said. "I'm definitely interested."

"Great. How do you feel about starting tomorrow morning? I can train you right away."

"Tomorrow morning is fine. What time should I arrive?"

"Nine o'clock. Do you remember where the restaurant is?" Michael inquired.

"Yes."

"Then I'll see you tomorrow morning, Jeannie."

"Goodbye," Jeannie said before hanging up. She smiled widely, feeling a lot more confident than she had an hour ago.

"Hey, Mom! Guess what?" Jeannie yelled as she ran down the stairs.

* * *

Part Two:

❧

Graduates

The months of May and June went in fast for Jeannie, Pamela and Lila. They were all excited about the end of senior year and could feel the approaching change.

Jeannie was busy working at Michael's restaurant. The work was tiring and the hours were long, but Jeannie was making a lot of money. She loved the feeling of freedom that the money gave her. It also made Jeannie happy to help her mother financially. Michael was a wonderful boss. He treated Jeannie like an equal and was very friendly.

Lila was glad her uncle hired Jeannie. Deep down, she couldn't help but feel like a proud mother. People had always told her that she'd make a wonderful mother one day, now she thought it might be true. The only thing she regretted about Jeannie's job was how little time it allowed for them to hang out. However, Lila was kept busy; she was trying to find employment as a photographer. She was starting to get worried about her photography career since she hadn't received a response from the university.

Pamela was ecstatic when, in late June, she received the offer of acceptance into Western Heights University. She was so excited that she had trouble concentrating on her final exams. Reconfirming Pamela's belief that she had the world's best friends, Jeannie and Lila formed a study group with her. Although they could've been easily distracted by each other's company, Jeannie, Pamela and Lila studied hard. They knew they'd have fun at their graduation party.

* * *

The night of their graduation party, Lila, Jeannie and Pamela got ready in the Ford's master bedroom. Lila's parents had been kind enough to lend them their room which was now covered in clothing, jewelry and make-up.

"Come on, guys! Dad's waiting in the car," Lila urged her friends. She watched Pamela and Jeannie as they playfully fought for the last look in the mirror. "You both look fine," she reassured them.

"We better," Jeannie replied as she put on one last coat of red lipstick. "Perfection is expected."

"By who?" Pamela interjected. "There's no such thing as perfection."

Pamela's words were a lie as each girl looked silently into the mirror.

Jeannie's hair was curled and styled in a fashionable manner. She wore a pale blue dress and had a lot of silver jewelry around her neck and wrists.

Pamela wore a silky black Spanish-styled dress that swayed magnificently every time she moved. Although she didn't like to admit that appearances mattered, she knew that tonight she looked like a million dollars.

Lila wore a short dark green dress that had black lace over it. The dress brought out the sparkle in her green eyes and showed off her athletic frame. She completed her appearance with chunky, yet feminine, jewelry.

Honk. Honk. Honk. Lila's dad urged them to hurry up as he pressed the car's horn.

The three girls quickly turned their gaze from the mirror and then hurried down the stairs. Lila's mom took a few pictures of them before they dashed outside to the waiting car.

"This place looks amazing," Lila commented as she stepped into the hall Western Heights High School had rented. "I wish I could photograph every brilliant detail of it."

Adorned with dark rugs, dazzling chandeliers and long cloth-covered tables which elegantly displayed food, the hall was indeed beautiful.

"Lila, we're here to party, not work," Jeannie said with a giggle.

"Photography is not work in my eyes," Lila replied defensively. "It's who I am."

Jeannie turned her eyes away from Lila and to the string of pale orange lights hanging from the ceiling. She was upset by Lila's reaction to her comment.

"Who wants to make a fool of themselves on the dance floor with me?" Pamela inquired, noticing the rising tension.

"Count me in," Jeannie replied, glad for the distraction.

"Count me out," Lila said, shaking her head. "I would rather watch the sea of dancers than join in."

"Please join us," Jeannie begged, pulling at Lila's arm.

"I said no," Lila snapped, jerking her arm away from Jeannie's grasp.

Pamela was surprised by Lila's behavior, but not as shocked as Jeannie looked.

"Okay," Jeannie muttered, leading Pamela onto the dance floor and joining a group of dancers.

Jeannie forced herself to dance to the music, but she wasn't having fun. She was too busy wondering what Lila's problem was.

Lila felt awful about her reaction to Jeannie's gesture. She hadn't meant to be rude. She just felt a lot of pressure, and most of it was coming from the fact she hadn't received any word from Western Heights University. She turned her attention away from the dance floor, directing it towards the refreshment table instead.

"Can I buy you something to eat or drink?" a voice asked from behind Lila.

Lila spun around to see Doug Kenningson standing behind her. She looked over his broad shoulders in search of Jeannie. Lila knew Jeannie had been too shy to talk to Doug during the school year, but perhaps she would be more confident now.

"Um, Lila," Doug muttered, waving his hand in front of her face.

"What?" Lila asked, giving up on her unsuccessful search for Jeannie.

"I asked if I could buy you something to eat or drink," Doug answered uncomfortably.

"The food and drinks are free," Lila responded, casting Doug a strange look.

"I know that. I was trying to be funny, but I see the joke lost its momentum some time ago."

"Yeah," Lila said slowly, wondering why Doug was talking to her.

On the dance floor, Jeannie spun around to cast a quick glance in Lila's direction. She was surprised to see that Lila wasn't where they had left her. Jeannie felt the music surge through her body as she closed her eyes and danced to her favorite song.

"Hey! Why is Lila talking to Doug Kenningson?"

Jeannie's eyes flew open upon hearing Pamela's words. She looked where Pamela pointed and gasped. Lila and Doug were less than fifty feet away from her. They looked like they were having a serious conversation – a conversation intimate friends might have. However, Jeannie knew that Lila and Doug weren't friends; they hardly even knew each other.

Jeannie marched angrily towards Lila and Doug, despite Pamela's protest. She had to find out what they were talking about. As Jeannie approached the suspicious-looking scene, she heard Doug say, "I've liked you for a while, Lila."

Lila looked at Doug in shock. "What did you just say?"

"I said I've liked you for a long time. I didn't have the nerve to tell you before now."

Wide-eyed, Lila gazed at Doug. She had no idea Jeannie was listening to their conversation.

"You...you hardly know me," Lila stuttered.

"No," Doug admitted, "but I would like to. You seem like a really cool girl. I admire the work you did for the school's recycling program."

"Oh, thank you!" Lila said sincerely. Getting permission to install three compost bins on the school's outdoor property hadn't been an easy task, and she was happy that someone recognized all the hard work she'd done.

"So, would you like to go out sometime?"

"No!" Jeannie cried, appearing from behind Doug. "She has a severe dating phobia. Men scare her something fierce. Sorry, Doug!"

"Oh, I'm sorry to hear that. I hope you get over your, um, phobia," Doug said, his face noticeably red even in the dim lighting.

"Jeannie!" Lila finally exclaimed after Doug had hurried away.

"Lila!" Jeannie yelled back. "What the hell was that all about?"

"Nothing," Lila replied, waving her hand in the air to symbolize that Doug professing his desire for her was no big deal. She hoped that Jeannie wasn't too upset by his words.

"Ha!" Jeannie laughed scornfully. "First you flirt with my man, and then you lie to me about it. What's gotten into you?"

"Me?" Lila asked in shock. "What's gotten into you is the better question. I wasn't flirting with him. He came to me."

"You must've been giving him signals," Jeannie protested while tears stung her eyes. "Why else would he ask you out?"

Lila felt tears brimming in her eyes now. She was shaken by Jeannie's comment. "I didn't give him any signals," Lila said meekly. "I looked for you when Doug first approached me."

Jeannie felt her heart break a little by Lila's comment. She instantly wished she could take back all the mean things which were said. *I should have trusted Lila. I know she would never entice any guy that I liked.* Jeannie felt like hugging Lila and telling her that she was sorry. However, she had already dug herself in too deep. Jeannie knew she would look like a fool if she apologized in front of all the people who'd gathered around to watch Lila and her fight.

"Well, you didn't try very hard," Jeannie finally replied. Her tone of voice lacked the vigor it had just moments ago.

"I didn't lead Doug on," Lila told Pamela in a hurt tone as she watched Jeannie storm away. A few tears fell down her cheeks, making her mascara run.

"I know," Pamela said soothingly.

"Then why doesn't Jeannie realize it?"

"Jeannie jumped to conclusions when she heard Doug asking you out. You know how much she likes him. She probably didn't want to believe that he likes you and not her."

"This is so stupid," Lila said grumpily, turning her back to Pamela and facing the refreshment table. "I don't even like the guy."

Pamela understood that Lila needed some time alone. She looked around the room, but she couldn't find Jeannie. "I guess I'll be dancing by myself," Pamela muttered as she headed towards the dance floor. Although Pamela was surrounded by her classmates, she had never felt so lonely in her life.

Across the hall, Jeannie stood alone and dejected in a carpeted bathroom. She wiped away a tear, unsure if she was crying over her unrequited love for Doug or the way she'd just treated her best friend. Jeannie didn't want to face the world outside the bathroom. She wanted to go home.

Jeannie finally crept out of the bathroom, through the mass of people and into an empty room. The sudden silence sounded foreign to her ears. The area in which she stood seemed to be a storage room for chairs and tables. Downtrodden, Jeannie took a chair from a nearby stack and then sat down.

"Have any of you seen Jeannie Dallas?" Pamela asked a group of girls who stood near the punch bowl. The girls shook their heads and then resumed chatting. Pamela felt like screaming. It had been an hour since the incident with Doug and no one had seen Jeannie. Adding to Pamela's annoyance was the fact that Lila refused to look for Jeannie.

Lila was silently following Pamela as her friend inquired about Jeannie's whereabouts. Although she wouldn't admit it, Lila was starting to get concerned as well. Her father would be here any minute to pick them up, and he would be furious that they allowed Jeannie to wander off by herself at a party. She knew he was always overly protective of her and her friends.

"I think I see her," Pamela said suddenly, interrupting Lila's thoughts.

Lila looked where Pamela was pointing and noticed Jeannie, who was now sulking near the exit door.

"Yeah, that's her," Lila replied, trying to keep her voice neutral. However, she couldn't help the feeling of relief that spread throughout her body.

"Lila's dad is here," Jeannie said sheepishly when her two angry-looking friends arrived.

The ride home was very quiet.

I've never been so embarrassed, Jeannie silently cringed.

I can't believe Jeannie has the nerve to treat me this way, Lila seethed.

How could Jeannie run off during the party and leave me to worry? Pamela asked herself angrily.

"So, how was the dance?" Mr. Ford asked when they were almost at Pamela's house. He could sense the tension between his daughter and her friends, and he didn't want to cause uproar by asking too many questions. However, he didn't want to seem too uninterested either. In the end, "how was the dance?" seemed to be the most appropriate thing to ask.

"It was fine, Dad," Lila answered when no one else offered a reply.

"It was great," Jeannie added in a fake tone. "We're just tired from all the fun we had."

* * *

Part Three:

೧

The Darkest Hour

It was Saturday morning – the day after that horrible graduation party – and Jeannie had to be at work for 11 AM. She wished she could stay in bed all day, but she'd feel too guilty about letting another Ford down. It was 10 AM when Jeannie dialed Lila's telephone number.

"Hello?" Mr. Ford answered.

"Hi," Jeannie said politely. "Is Lila there?"

"She is," Mr. Ford said hesitantly.

Jeannie's heart began to race. *Did Lila tell her dad what happened at the dance? Did she tell him that she didn't want to speak to me?*

"She was asleep the last time I checked," Mr. Ford continued. "That was only a few minutes ago, so she's still probably sleeping."

Jeannie let out a sigh of relief. Although Lila may be a sleepyhead, she wasn't trying to avoid her.

"Would you like me to give her a message?" Mr. Ford offered.

"No, thanks, I'll call when I get back from work."

"Is my brother working you into the ground already?" he asked with a laugh.

"Not at all! He's a great boss."

"I'm glad to hear that. When Lila gets up, I'll let her know you called."

"Thanks, Mr. Ford. Have a nice day."

"You too, Jeannie. Goodbye."

"Bye."

Jeannie wished she'd got the chance to talk to Lila. She knew she'd be obsessing about the apology to her all day long. She tried, unsuccessfully, to push the thoughts out of her mind as she hurried to get ready for work.

"Hey, Lila, wake up," Mr. Ford urged his daughter while standing over her bed. "It's 11:30 – way past the time you should've been up."

"Ugh," Lila moaned. "Why do I have to wake up?"

"Half of the day is already gone. You can't stay in bed forever."

"Yes, I can," Lila replied in a groggy voice while placing a pillow over her head.

"No, you can't," Mr. Ford replied, taking the pillow away from Lila. "I need your help in the garden. At this rate, I'll never get your mother's pond installed."

"Fine," Lila muttered, forcing herself out of bed.

"I'll be in the garden. Join me once you've eaten breakfast, um, lunch."

Lila groaned deeply.

"Get your act together," Mr. Ford teased. "You should be more like Jeannie. She's already at work and you've hardly got up!"

"How would you know?" Lila snapped, annoyed at hearing Jeannie's name.

"She called almost two hours ago," Mr. Ford replied as he left Lila's room.

"Whatever," Lila muttered. She was sick of feeling so emotional. She decided to simply push it to the back of her mind.

Lila ran downstairs. She didn't realize it earlier, but she was pretty hungry. She'd just put two slices of bread into the toaster when a loud bang from the mailbox made her jump. Lila ran to the mailbox at the front door and flung it open. Inside was a large envelope from Western Heights University.

Lila quickly tore the package open and spread its contents onto the kitchen table. She skipped over the numerous brochures, paying particular attention to a one page typed letter. Lila picked up the letter and read quickly.

Dear Ms. Lila Ford. We are pleased to offer you unconditional admission to Western Heights University. Your impressive portfolio has gained you a place in the photography program. Please review the enclosed brochures for important information regarding your program. Congratulations and welcome to our fine institution.

Running outside, Lila screamed, "Dad!"

"What's wrong?" Mr. Ford asked when he saw his daughter frantically waving to him.

"Nothing's wrong!" Lila cried as she ran to her father and threw her arms around him. "Everything's wonderful!"

"Get off me, Lila," Mr. Ford said jokingly. "I'm covered in dirt." He tried to look stern but he couldn't stop the smile which played upon his lips. Although Mr. Ford had no clue what had excited Lila so much, his daughter's happiness never ceased to make him smile.

"I..." Lila said slowly, pausing for dramatic effect, "just got unconditional acceptance into Western Heights University for the specialized photography program!" Lila held the piece of paper for her dad to read. However, her hands were shaking so much that Mr. Ford could hardly see the words.

"Oh, that is wonderful!" Mr. Ford cried, wrapping his daughter in a hug.

"I thought you said you were covered in dirt," Lila pointed out with a laugh.

"To hell with the dirt! My baby just got accepted into university!"

"Not just any university," Lila corrected her dad after breaking from the embrace. "Western Heights University is acclaimed for having the best art programs in the entire country. Do you know how many people must have applied to the photography program? I bet there were thousands! I'm so lucky to get accepted."

"Luck had nothing to do with it," Mr. Ford said proudly. "You have a natural talent which you strengthened through hard work. You should be so proud of yourself."

"I am," Lila said happily as she stared at her acceptance letter. "Where's Mom? I can't wait to tell her the good news."

"She's at the grocery store, but she should be back soon."

"I'm going to read everything the university sent me," Lila said with a wide smile as she hurried towards the house. "Oh, you needed my help with the pond, right?" she asked grudgingly.

"No. The pond can wait. I'll get cleaned up and join you inside. I want to know all about Western Heights University and the photography program."

Lila couldn't wipe the smile off her face as she gathered all the information from the university and then headed to the living room.

* * *

It was late at night when Michael flipped the sign on his restaurant door to "closed."

"Are you tired?" Michael asked, slumping into a chair beside Jeannie.

"Sort of," Jeannie admitted timidly. Although she thought of herself and Michael as good friends, she still wanted to make a good impression on him. After all, Michael was first and foremost her boss.

"Come on, Jeannie," Michael said with a playful smirk as he punched her gently on the shoulder. "There's no need to lie to me. You're exhausted, aren't you?"

"Well, yes," Jeannie finally admitted.

"Today was a very busy day – that's why I asked you to do overtime."

"Yeah, it was packed."

"No one can resist my homemade lasagna," Michael said cockily.

"It is very good."

"Then you'll have dinner with me? I have half of a lasagna dish left over. If I slip it into the oven now, it'll be ready in five minutes."

"Thanks," Jeannie replied. "I'd love some."

"Make yourself at home, Jeannie. I'll be back in five."

Jeannie cast Michael a grateful smile as she leaned back in the chair.

"Here we are," Michael said, returning with two plates of food a few minutes later.

"This looks great," Jeannie commented before lifting a forkful of lasagna. "And tastes even better," she added after sampling the food.

"I'm glad you like it."

They ate the rest of the meal in silence. Afterwards, Jeannie took Michael's plate and stood up.

Michael took the plate back from Jeannie. "Sit down and relax."

"Okay," Jeannie replied as she sat back down. She was starting to feel a little uncomfortable. Something was different about Michael.

"Your restaurant really is a success," Jeannie commented, trying to turn the conversation into a more professional one.

Michael laughed. "Yeah, and I'm grateful for it. I'd be devastated if I couldn't own this place."

"Did you always want your own restaurant?"

"Yes, cooking is my passion. I didn't want to work for someone else though. I wanted to be my own boss so I could cook whatever I wanted."

"How did you know cooking was your passion?" Jeannie inquired, leaning forward in anticipation. "When did you know what you'd do for the rest of your life?"

"I've known since I was ten."

"But how?"

"I was the only kid who actually wanted to cook dinner."

Jeannie slumped back in her chair. "I wish I knew what my calling was."

"You'll figure it out someday but don't be in a big rush to do so. Having an all-consuming passion isn't that great. Heck, my passion and drive have kept me unmarried for thirty-six years. A life full of dedication can be a lonely one, Jeannie. I wouldn't want to see that happen to you."

"Thanks for saying that," Jeannie said sincerely. "You've made things a little clearer for me."

"I'm glad I could help," Michael said with a lopsided smile as he leaned in closer to Jeannie. "You know you're beautiful, right?"

Jeannie uttered a small gasp, shocked to hear those words come from Michael's mouth. He'd never spoken to her like that before.

"You don't have to say anything," Michael muttered softly.

"I'm...I'm just surprised to hear you say, well, what you just said," Jeannie stammered, feeling her face flush deeply.

"You are?" Michael asked with wide eyes and raised eyebrows. "I can't believe that for a second, Jeannie. Your beauty is so apparent that boys must tell you how much they admire you."

Jeannie couldn't help but snort slightly at Michael's comment. "Hardly," she remarked, while thoughts of Doug circulated in her mind. "My heart was broken last night."

"What man would break your heart? He must've been blind."

"Actually, he isn't. He preferred Lila over me." Jeannie felt anger boil inside her.

"That must hurt," Michael said with a little too much sympathy. "But I've got to say that Lila has nothing on you. Don't get me wrong, Lila is a pretty girl who I love very much, but she's definitely not a woman like you."

"We're...we're the same age," Jeannie stuttered in embarrassment.

"You've matured faster, Jeannie."

"Um, okay, I think I better go."

"No. Sit down, Jeannie. We've worked together for two months but I feel like I hardly know you. I would love to know you on a more personal level."

"I don't know what you're implying and I don't want to know. I have to go." Jeannie's heart pounded as she hurried to get her jacket from the employee's closet. When she turned around, Michael was blocking the path to the door. "Excuse me," she said shakily, trying to push past him.

Michael grasped Jeannie by the shoulders. "Don't go like this, Jeannie. I feel like you're mad at me."

"I'm not mad," Jeannie reassured Michael. "I just think it's best for me to go now."

"You *are* mad at me," Michael insisted. "I can tell that you are."

"I'll be mad if you don't let me go," Jeannie said through clenched teeth. "Now please move out of my way."

Michael obediently let go of Jeannie's shoulders and stepped backwards. "It's dark outside. Do you want a ride home?"

"No."

"Are you sure? It'll be no trouble."

"I'm sure." Jeannie felt her heart race as she slipped her jacket on and then watched her keys fall out of the pocket.

"I'll get them for you," Michael offered.

"No, I can get them."

Jeannie bent down to pick up the keys just as he did the same thing. She was caught off guard as Michael grabbed her and then pressed his lips against hers. It was a horrid, choking feeling made all the worse by his stubble that scratched her face. She even smelled nauseating grease and cooking products on him.

"Get off me!" Jeannie demanded as she pushed Michael away.

Michael refused to let go of Jeannie. Instead, he tried to kiss her again.

"Stop it!" Jeannie cried as his grip tightened.

"I can't. You're so beautiful, Jeannie."

"What's gotten into you?" Jeannie yelled as she struggled to free herself from Michael's grasp.

34

"Nothing has changed. If you give me what I want, you can have this job forever. If you don't, I'll fire you. You don't want that, do you, Jeannie? I know that you need the money. I've always thought you were hot, and I know that you like me too. You're always flirting with me."

"I was just being friendly!"

"Bull, Jeannie, I know you like me."

"I hate you!" Jeannie screamed. Summoning all her strength, she pushed Michael backwards and then ran out of the restaurant.

The only light came from the streetlamps. Jeannie was hurrying to the bus stop, but she didn't know why. She knew she wouldn't be able to get on the bus when it came. Jeannie's face was streaked with tears. Her body trembled as she thought about what had happened. Not only had she been sexually harassed, the person who had done it to her was someone she trusted and respected. Jeannie felt like being sick when she thought about the kiss Michael had forced upon her. The sound of him calling her name kept running through her mind. Although he was now blocks away from her, Jeannie knew he was with her right now.

Jeannie forced herself to stop trembling. *I won't be a victim,* she told herself. *I have done nothing wrong. It's all Michael Ford's fault. Michael Ford,* Jeannie repeated in shock. She temporarily forgot that Michael was Lila's beloved uncle. The thought made her sick to the stomach again.

Jeannie wiped her tears as she approached the bus stop. A man and woman were waiting for a bus as well. From the streetlamp's glow, she could tell that they were looking at her. She felt like screaming, "What are you looking at? Can you tell that I've just been sexually harassed?"

The bus took ages to come. During that time, Jeannie's mind was working overtime. She knew that she had to tell her mom. She was even considering telling the police. What upset Jeannie even more than the assault was the fact that Michael really hadn't hurt her – physically, at least. Jeannie wondered if Michael would get into trouble. The thought that he might get away scot-free made Jeannie's stomach churn.

After the seemingly longest bus ride of her life, Jeannie finally arrived home. She opened the door and stepped inside. She'd hoped to be met with darkness but was disappointed when she found the living room light on.

"Jeannie?" Mrs. Dallas asked as she emerged from the living room. "Why are you just standing there? Is everything alright?"

"I'm okay," Jeannie began to say. However, her words were so far from the truth that she immediately broke down in tears.

"Oh, dear!" Mrs. Dallas exclaimed as she raced to her fallen daughter's side. "What is it? What's happened?"

"Michael, my boss, he…"

"He what?" Mrs. Dallas demanded.

"He…he…" Jeannie stammered, feeling frightened by her mother's harsh, anxious tone.

"Whatever happened, it'll be okay. You need to tell me what's going on though."

"Michael forced himself on me," Jeannie said through tears. She was angry at herself for feeling embarrassed and ashamed. Jeannie knew she was blameless but she couldn't get the negative self-perception out of her thoughts. She hated Michael fiercely for what he was still doing to her.

"Are you alright?" Mrs. Dallas asked slowly with wide, terrified eyes.

"I think so. I'm physically alright, but he scared me so much. He wouldn't let me go. He kissed me and tried to make me stay with him. I was able to escape though."

"He held you against your will?" Mrs. Dallas asked with a stern face.

"Yes. I told him no, but he wouldn't listen."

"What would he have done if you hadn't got away?"

"Mom! That's a horrible thing to ask!"

"I need to know, Jeannie."

"Michael said he would fire me if I didn't do what he said."

"Okay," Mrs. Dallas said as steadily as she could. "We're going to the police station and filing a report." She offered her hand to her daughter. Slowly, Jeannie reached for it. "We can do this," Mrs. Dallas reassured her. "Everything will be alright. I know you must want to forget about tonight but you have to tell the police."

"I know," Jeannie said as she embraced her mother, "but it's just so hard. I looked up to Michael."

"Try your best to be strong, my darling, but always know that I'll be strong enough for the both of us. I'm here to help you through this, to make you understand that this wasn't your fault."

"I know it's not my fault," Jeannie said.

"Good. That realization is your key to recovery."

"I'm not sick, Mom."

"Well, I certainly am," Mrs. Dallas muttered.

The night seemed to go on forever. Jeannie and Mrs. Dallas had to wait several minutes before talking privately with a police officer.

Jeannie dreaded reliving the night's events, but she did her best to recall every detail accurately.

It was a night that Jeannie wished to forget. She knew, however, that the horrible events wouldn't soon be forgotten. She also knew that the worst was yet to come; the Ford family was bound to find out what had happened.

Jeannie had terrifying dreams that night. She dreamt that she hadn't escaped from Michael. She woke up in a cold sweat to find her mother sleeping in a nearby chair. Jeannie managed to smile weakly at her before closing her eyes.

* * *

Ring. Ring. Ring.

"I'll get the telephone," Mrs. Dallas said.

Jeannie looked up from her cold cereal and nodded. Although it was 11 AM, she and her mom were just eating breakfast. They had awoken late due to the emotionally draining events of yesterday.

"Yes, she's here," Mrs. Dallas said after answering the telephone. "One moment please."

Jeannie looked up at her mom with wide eyes. "Who is it?" she asked fearfully, praying that it wasn't Michael.

"It's the police officer you talked to yesterday."

Jeannie gulped before getting up and taking the telephone. "Hello?"

"Hello, Ms. Dallas. This is Officer Reynolds. I reviewed the details of your complaint and would like to know whether or not you plan on pressing charges against Michael Ford."

38

"I want to press charges." Jeannie was surprised to hear herself sound so confident.

"Okay, Ms. Dallas, I'll be in touch with you shortly."

"Thank you," Jeannie said before hanging up the telephone.

"What did Officer Reynolds say?" Mrs. Dallas asked.

"He wanted to know if I was going to press charges. I said yes. Did I do the right thing?"

"Yes," Mrs. Dallas said firmly. "You were sexually harassed and wrongfully terminated from your job."

"Ugh!" Jeannie moaned as she placed her hands against her head. "I think I'm doing the right thing but I'm not sure. I feel so confused and overwhelmed. I'm dreading going to see the Fords today."

"You're going to see Lila and her parents?" Mrs. Dallas asked in surprise.

"Yes," Jeannie replied. "They will find out anyway and I want them to hear it from me. I'm the innocent party here and I want them to know it. I don't want Michael telling them lies about what happened."

"Do you think he would?"

"I don't know. Everything I thought Michael was – a respectable man and a trusted friend – was wrong. I feel as if he's capable of anything now."

"Do you want me to come with you?" Mrs. Dallas offered.

"No. Things might get ugly."

"Just remember that you did nothing wrong."

"I know that. You know that. Heck, even Michael must know that. But Michael is Mr. Ford's brother and Lila's uncle. They're sure to believe him, or at the very least, blame me for his actions."

"Women can't be blamed for men's inappropriate actions. We're not only getting justice for you, Jeannie, we're going to empower every wrongfully treated woman."

"One step at a time," Jeannie muttered as she got up from the kitchen table. "Will you drive me to Lila's?"

Silence filled the Dallas' car as they drove to the Ford's house. Dark clouds now covered the sky and it had started to rain.

"Are you sure you don't want me to come in with you?" Mrs. Dallas asked.

"No. I need to do this by myself," Jeannie said assertively. "I'll call you once I'm done," she added before getting out of the car and heading towards the Ford's house. She rang the doorbell and then waited anxiously.

"Jeannie!" Lila exclaimed as she opened the door. "Come in."

Jeannie stepped into the house, seeing it now as the house that belonged to Michael's brother. She hoped she could see it as she once used to – as her best friend's house where numerous slumber parties and chat sessions had taken place.

"I'm glad you came," Lila said. "I want to talk about what happened at the graduation dance."

"The graduation dance?" Jeannie repeated as she furrowed her eyebrows. "Oh," she muttered, suddenly realizing that Lila was talking about the harsh words which they'd exchanged over Doug. With all that had happened since then, Doug and a silly dance were the last things on her mind.

"I want you to know that I forgive you – that's if you want to be forgiven. I understand that you were upset, but I have no feelings for Doug and I never gave him any reason to believe otherwise."

"I'm sorry," Jeannie said quickly. "I shouldn't have said what I did and now I realize that you're completely blameless. Listen, Lila, I have something really important to tell you."

"No. *I* have something really important to tell *you*," Lila said with a wide smile. She felt relieved that their friendship was back on the right track.

"What is it?" Jeannie asked as she swallowed the imaginary lump in her throat.

"I got accepted into Western Heights University's photography program!"

"Whoa, that's great," Jeannie said with as much enthusiasm as she could muster. However, she soon realized her enthusiasm wasn't enough as Lila's happy expression faded slightly.

"I got an unconditional acceptance. That means I'll be going to university for sure!"

"That's really great," Jeannie replied in the same monotone. She was too busy thinking about that horrible night to fully concentrate on her friend's words. As impossible as it seemed, being with Lila somehow made the situation even worse.

"What's wrong with you?" Lila finally exploded. "Why can't you even pretend to be happy for me?"

"I...I am," Jeannie stuttered.

"Bull. You didn't even crack a smile when I told you the good news."

"How can you expect me to smile?" Jeannie asked with rising anger. "Your perverted uncle sexually harassed me so badly that I had to call the police!" As soon as the words left her mouth, Jeannie knew she could've found a better way to inform Lila of her uncle's misdeeds.

"He did *what?*" Mr. Ford cried out in shock.

Jeannie looked at the top of the stairs to see Mr. Ford standing there as if he was frozen. *He must have come down to see what all the yelling was about,* she realized. *I bet he never expected to hear what he just did.*

"This...this has to be some sort of sick joke," Lila stuttered as her face became pale.

"Oh, Jeannie," Mr. Ford said apologetically as he reached her side. "I have no clue what Michael has done to you, but whatever it is, I'm so sorry. He was always bad-tempered but I never thought he'd hurt anyone. He didn't hurt you, did he?"

"Michael hurt me in the worst way possible," Jeannie admitted. "He betrayed my trust and friendship."

"Tell me everything that happened," Lila demanded, still trying to comprehend her friend's words. It wasn't as if she didn't believe her. She was just surprised that her father was so quick to believe Jeannie without hearing the full story first.

"I was working overtime last night," Jeannie began to describe the terrible event again. "When Michael closed the restaurant, he insisted on making me dinner. After dinner, I wanted to go home but he wouldn't let me leave. He said some very inappropriate things, kissed me, held me against my will and then fired me when I refused to do what he wanted."

Lila looked at Jeannie compassionately. "Oh, Jeannie," she said, embracing her friend. "I am so sorry. I feel so guilty."

"Don't you dare blame yourself," Jeannie scolded.

"I was the one who got you the job in the first place. Why would Michael do this?"

"I don't know," Mr. Ford answered in disgust, "but he's no brother of mine."

"I'm pressing charges. This must be horrible for you both to hear, but I wanted you to know the truth."

"The truth will set you free," Lila mumbled ironically.

"If the truth really sets you free, why do I feel a heavy weight in my stomach?" Jeannie asked.

"The truth is heavier to bear than fiction," Mr. Ford responded. "That's why it's so important." Sickened, he left the room.

Jeannie and Lila didn't talk about the incident with Michael any further. Jeannie refused to allow him to take up any more of her time. Instead, she insisted on hearing about Lila's acceptance into Western Heights University. As Lila talked about the photography program, Jeannie suddenly remembered that she was now unemployed. The last thing she wanted to do was go job hunting. However, she knew it was the one thing she needed to do.

* * *

As Officer Reynolds had promised, he called Jeannie promptly with an update on her case. With her mother by her side, Jeannie sat on her bedroom floor and listened. The telephone was pressed hard against her ear and her hand gripped it tightly.

"Michael Ford's been arrested for sexual assault," Officer Reynolds informed her. "This case will go to court and you'll be required to testify. It's advised that you seek legal representation. In the meantime, you may want to obtain a restraining order against Mr. Ford since he has posted bail."

Jeannie suddenly felt numb. She wanted nothing more than to crawl into bed and pretend none of this had ever happened. However, Jeannie knew she had to stay strong and face this situation.

* * *

It was a sunny morning on the sixth of July as Jeannie and her mom sat in the kitchen. Slowly and silently, they ate breakfast while thinking about recent events.

For the past two days, Michael had stood trial for sexual assault and wrongful termination. Much to Jeannie's fury, he had pleaded not guilty to both charges. As Jeannie stood in a court filled with strangers and relived the most horrific night of her life, she felt exposed and embarrassed. Even worse was how long the jury took to reach a verdict. As the hours ticked by slowly, Jeannie anxiously wondered if they didn't believe her. When the jury finally announced that they'd found Michael guilty of both charges, Jeannie broke into tears of relief.

"How are you doing, honey?" Mrs. Dallas finally interrupted the silence.

"I'm alright," Jeannie replied truthfully.

"I'm so proud of how you handled yourself in court."

"Thanks, but it was my lawyer who won the case for me."

"Justice was served," Mrs. Dallas pointed out. "That's the important thing."

"I got my justice," Jeannie agreed as she thought about Michael's six month prison sentence, "but I haven't helped any other ill-treated women."

"Wasn't it you who said one step at a time?" Mrs. Dallas reminded her daughter.

Jeannie nodded. "I'm going to stand by those words."

"Don't forget to have fun as well. You certainly deserve it."

"Thanks, Mom," Jeannie said as she got up from the kitchen table and washed her bowl. "I think I'll see Pamela and Lila today. We haven't hung out together in a while."

"That sounds like a nice idea," Mrs. Dallas said as she stood up. "As for me, I better get to work."

"Hey, Mom?" Jeannie said suddenly.

"Yes, dear?"

"Thank you."

"For what?" Mrs. Dallas asked in surprise.

"For standing by me these past few weeks, and for always taking care of me."

"That's what mothers do, Jeannie."

"You've gone beyond the call of duty," Jeannie argued as she kissed her mom on the cheek and then scurried out of the kitchen.

* * *

Part Four:

℘

Unleashed

"I haven't taken many photographs this summer," Lila stated as she, Jeannie and Pamela sat around the Mitchell's pool later that day. "It's already July and I've hardly picked up my camera for anything other than my mom's birthday party. I'm going to be rusty when school starts."

"You could never be rusty," Jeannie pointed out. "You have an innate talent for photography."

"Jeannie's right," Pamela agreed. "Those shots you took at your mom's party were amazing."

"Do you really think so?" Lila asked shyly.

"Yes," Pamela answered. "Who else but you would think of composing a photo as seen entirely through a large, transparent balloon?"

"That shot was pretty good," Lila admitted with a smile. "I don't want to talk about my photos in a past tense though. I want to get some new shots."

"What kind of things do you want to shoot?" Jeannie asked, making her way to the pool's edge and then dabbling her feet in the cool water.

"Since I love wildlife and the woods, I want to stick with that. The problem is I've photographed all the nearby parks. I want to shoot at a new location."

"Then why don't you?" Pamela pressed. "There are some really beautiful conservation parks just outside the city."

"I know that," Lila replied. "But my parents work full-time and I don't have a car."

"We can take mine," Pamela offered.

"Since when did you have a car?" Jeannie interrupted.

"Well, I didn't exactly get a car. I just got the rights to one. My parents said I could use the second car whenever I wanted."

"Do I sense a road trip?" Lila asked with sparkling eyes.

"Sounds good to me," Jeannie responded. "I have no responsibilities."

"Let's go to The Grove Conservation Park," Lila suggested. "I've heard that it has everything from a sandy beach to hiking trails and even a partially equipped campsite."

"Sounds like you've done your research," Jeannie said with a laugh.

"Hold on, guys," Pamela protested. "I'd have to ask my parents if I'm allowed to take the car for an extended period of time."

"It would only be for a few days," Lila said.

"I'm in," Jeannie said quickly. "I need a break."

"Don't you realize that The Grove Conservation Park is probably fully booked?" Pamela pointed out.

"Maybe they are, but then again, maybe they're not," Lila said. "I could phone the park office and find out."

"It wouldn't hurt to ask," Pamela finally admitted. "You know where the telephone is, Lila. The phonebook is right beside it."

"Thanks," Lila said happily as she hurried into the house.

"You want to go camping as badly as Lila and I do," Jeannie said with a mischievous smile. "Admit it."

"Camping really isn't my thing. You know that I'm terrified of bears."

"I doubt you'll see any bears, Pam."

"And how would you know?"

Jeannie never got a chance to reply as Lila came back outside.

"The Grove Conservation Park has two campsites available," Lila informed them. "If we want one of the sites, we better book it soon."

"I'll have to check with my parents first," Pamela replied. "I'll talk to them tonight and then let you guys know soon after. In the meantime, I'm going swimming!"

"Hey!" Jeannie cried as Pamela jumped into the pool, causing water to splash over her.

"It's a pool – you're meant to get wet," Pamela responded with a giggle.

"Only if you're in it!" Jeannie cried.

"Then come in," Pamela urged teasingly as she pulled Jeannie into the water.

Ring. Ring. Ring.

"Hello?" Jeannie greeted as she picked up the telephone in the kitchen. She'd just returned from Pamela's house and was about to make dinner.

"Hey, Jeannie. It's Pamela."

"And Lila."

"Hey, guys," Jeannie replied. "The miracle of three-way calling, huh?"

"Definitely, and guess what else is a miracle?" Pamela joked.

"What?" Jeannie asked curiously.

"My parents said I can take the car!"

"I've booked a campsite for us," Lila added. "We have it from this Wednesday to Saturday. You can come, right?"

"Of course," Jeannie replied. "I wouldn't miss it for the world."

"I'll bring the tent, three sleeping bags and fold-up chairs," Lila offered, beginning to organize the camping necessities.

"I'll take care of the food and beverages," Jeannie added.

"And I'll drive us there," Pamela said. "This sounds great, doesn't it?"

"It sounds awesome!" Jeannie and Lila said simultaneously.

* * *

With Jeannie and Lila in tow, Pamela drove her family car throughout a scenic countryside. Lush green trees lined the road and, with a careful eye, birds could be seen nesting in the branches. The air smelled fresh and there were small white clouds in the bright blue sky. The atmosphere differed vastly from the bustle of the city and was readily welcomed by the girls.

"Are we there yet?" Lila inquired.

"No," Pamela replied through a sigh. "Would you stop asking me that? You sound like my little brother."

"Sorry," Lila mumbled. "I'm just so anxious to get to The Grove Conservation Park. My camera is itching to start clicking."

"We'll have to set up camp first," Jeannie reminded her friend.

"Alright, but then I'll take pictures."

"Then we'll make lunch," Jeannie corrected. "I'm starting to get hungry."

They were silent for the rest of the car ride. Pamela concentrated on driving while listening to the soft music coming from the car's speakers. Lila and Jeannie occupied themselves by looking out the windows.

"We're here," Pamela announced as a wooden sign which read The Grove Conservation Park loomed high in front of the car. She brought the car to a stop and then rolled down the window. "Hello," she greeted the girl in the wooden hut. "We're here for the four day reservation booked by Dallas, Ford and Mitchell."

"Just a moment, please," the park employee said before disappearing from Pamela's view. She returned a minute later with a handful of brochures. "You're at campsite twenty-one," she said with a friendly smile. "To get to your campsite, keep going straight and then turn right at the first stop. From there you'll reach your destination in about five minutes. Your campsite comes equipped with a toilet, a change room and water facilities. Here is some literature on our fine park. These brochures will provide you with an overview of the park, interesting facts and a map. If you have any questions, don't hesitate to ask. This hut will be operated by a park employee from seven in the morning to eight at night."

"Thank you," Pamela said as she took the brochures and tried to remember everything the employee had said.

"No, thank you," the employee said with a wide smile. "I hope you have the most wonderful time. I'm sure you'll create memories that will last a lifetime."

"I'm sure we will," Pamela said with a straight face, while trying desperately not to laugh.

As Pamela drove the car away from the hut, she, Lila and Jeannie burst out laughing.

"Poor girl," Lila said through a giggle. "Her speech was so rehearsed."

"It's actually sad that she's told what to do," Pamela replied. "She's being drained of her own personality to suit the needs of her employer. Jobs in the service sector are so demeaning."

"Oh, man," Jeannie said while rolling her eyes. "It's just a summer job. Besides, the girl didn't look oppressed, drained or anything else negative."

"The corporate world works quietly, transforming their workers through time with low wages and subliminal messages."

"I love you, Pamela, but you're seriously paranoid," Jeannie said.

"I'm not paranoid, just observant."

"Let's leave all talk of society behind us," Lila suggested. "We should let the surrounding beauty fill our spirits and minds."

"I thought you were a photographer, not a poet," Pamela commented as she looked at Lila in the rearview mirror.

"I can be both," Lila defended herself.

"Here's our turn," Jeannie hurried to say.

Pamela turned the car right and onto a dirt path. The trees had grown less dense, allowing the presence of a blue lake to be seen in the distance.

"You guys don't think there are any bears in these woods, do you?" Pamela asked with wide eyes.

"I don't know," Lila said in a joking tone of voice. "It certainly looks like a bear haven to me."

"Let's see what the literature says," Jeannie suggested, while reaching for the brochures and skimming through them. "Hmmm….interesting."

"What?" Pamela demanded anxiously.

"It says here that bears roam freely at The Grove Conservation Park and that they are commonly seen."

"It does?" Pamela asked.

"Yup, the brochure advises campers to keep all food tightly sealed in a car," Jeannie continued. "It also says that although bear attacks are frequent in this part of the woods, they usually aren't fatal."

"What?" Pamela cried, swerving the car slightly to the left.

Jeannie burst out laughing. Lila joined in shortly after.

"Relax," Jeannie soothed her friend. "I made it all up."

"That's so not funny," Pamela whined. "You sounded so serious, as if you knew exactly what you were talking about."

"Blame it on the corporate world," Jeannie said jokingly. "I did work in the service sector, after all."

Everyone's attitude changed at the mention of Jeannie's job at Michael's restaurant. The atmosphere was one of tension, anger and even sadness.

"Hey! This is our campsite!" Pamela tried to say enthusiastically. However, her tone lacked sincerity.

Pamela stopped the car at campsite twenty-one and then exited the vehicle.

The area was quiet but not isolated. The campsites were about a hundred feet apart and separated by entrances to walking trails and, of course, trees.

"Let's get this up," Lila said as she slid the large, folded tent from its container. "Take this corner, Pam, and pull."

Pamela pulled on the tent's corner, causing it to open.

"Take these pegs and hammer them into the ground," Lila instructed Jeannie.

Jeannie did as she was told and then stood back to watch Lila assemble the tent's frame. After the poles were securely in place, it went up easily.

"The tent is really cool," Pamela commented as she crawled in.

"Thanks," Lila replied. "My family loves to go camping. We haven't been in over a year though."

"How come?" Jeannie inquired as she opened a can of soup and began heating it on Lila's portable stove.

"We've just been too busy, I guess. Mom has been working longer hours since the bank promoted her to a supervisor position. My dad is also over-worked at his marketing job."

"Those are busy jobs," Pamela stated as she stuck her head out of the tent. "Do you find it funny that your career will be so different from your parents? After all, photography is usually a lonely job that requires patience until that perfect shot arrives."

"When I first got interested in photography, I thought about that a lot," Lila admitted. "I knew that a photographer was a much different job than a bank supervisor or marketer. That's just another reason why I was drawn to the profession. I want a career that allows me to leave the stress behind and focus on the important things in life."

"Soup's ready!" Jeannie called as she brought her friends a bowl each.

"Let's check out the beach," Lila suggested after lunch had been eaten and the dishes put away.

The three friends strolled away from their campsite, along a dirt path and then onto a golden sand beach. The afternoon sun beat down harshly, causing the breeze off the water to be a source of relief. Lila, Pamela and Jeannie said nothing as they walked barefoot on the sand. They were all content to be with one another in a relaxed manner.

"Look at those stones," Lila commented as she raised her camera to an area of the beach that was covered with colorful, glittering stones. She snapped a photograph and then proceeded towards them.

"They're weird," Jeannie said as she bent down and picked up a shiny one. The piles of stones in front of her were of numerous colors and scattered amongst the golden sand.

"Those look store bought," Pamela added as she ran her hand over the smooth stones.

"Why would someone leave them on the beach?" Lila began to ask. However, she didn't have time to finish her sentence as someone shouted in the distance.

"What are you doing?" a woman called as she ran down the beach and towards the three friends.

"I was just taking a photograph," Lila explained while looking at the woman and the camera which hung around her neck.

"What did you see?" the woman asked breathlessly.

"Just these stones," Lila answered.

"Oh," the woman said as she sighed with disappointment.

"Is everything alright?" Lila inquired with concern.

"Everything's fine. I'm sorry if I scared you girls. I was just surprised to see you around my trap."

"Your trap?" Pamela asked curiously while staring at the middle-aged woman with curly red hair.

"I see that you're a photographer," the woman commented to Lila while ignoring Pamela's question.

"Yes. Soon to be a professional," Lila replied proudly.

"Then you'll be here to photograph Bigfoot."

"Excuse me?" Lila choked out.

"Why else would you claim to be an up-and-coming photographer?" the woman demanded. "That title is reserved for the one who captures the infamous Bigfoot on camera."

"Hold on a minute," Lila protested. "I'm not here to photograph Bigfoot. Heck, I don't even believe in him! I'm here to take photographs of the scenery. I'm going to study photography at Western Heights University this fall – that's why I said I'll soon be a professional."

"That's impressive," the woman complimented sincerely.

"Thanks for saying so."

"Why did you put these stones here?" Pamela asked, causing Lila's self-confident smile to fade.

"To lure Bigfoot. He's rumored to be attracted to shiny objects. My name's Katherine and I am a photographer. I've been hired by a small company called the P.A.A. They've hired me to photograph the Bigfoot which has been seen in this very area."

"The P.A.A.?" Jeannie asked with furrowed eyebrows.

"The Paranormal Activity Association," Katherine explained. "If I get a clear shot of Bigfoot, I'll become the famous photographer that I've always wanted to be. I've been out here for a week now but haven't seen anything."

"Your dedication is commendable," Lila commented, "but wouldn't you further your career by photographing things that actually exist?"

"Bigfoot exists," Katherine said with certainty.

"How can you be sure?" Lila challenged.

"I've seen the photographs of Bigfoot that the P.A.A. has gathered over the last few months. Although the pictures are fuzzy, they are certainly of something abnormal."

"Do you really think these shiny stones will attract Bigfoot?" Jeannie asked as innocently as she could. However, she couldn't keep a cynical tone from seeping into her voice.

"Yes, I do," Katherine replied.

"But it hasn't worked so far?" Jeannie continued to pry.

"No."

Silence filled the air as they all looked awkwardly at the glistening stones.

"I need it to work," Katherine added quietly.

"Why?" Lila inquired as she stared at Katherine. She could tell from the lines on the woman's face that she'd had a hard life.

"I've been out of work for some time now," Katherine explained. "I used to work in a store as a sales representative, but I left that job a year ago to follow my true passion of photography. However, the road to achieving my dream hasn't been easy, and it doesn't look like it'll be getting any brighter. Being a freelance photographer is tough. I've worked for a few companies on a contract basis, but that hardly covers my bills. The P.A.A. is funding my search for Bigfoot. One of the reasons I took this job is because it means a steady income for a few weeks. The main reason I took this job, however, is because I want to take a photograph that will change people's beliefs. I want to do something special with my talent for photography."

"Taking a photograph of Bigfoot will certainly do that," Lila nodded with a half-smile. Although she thought Katherine was crazy for wasting her time trying to find Bigfoot, she couldn't help but admire her passion.

"I guess I'll gather up these stones," Katherine said as she kneeled on the sand and began placing them in a black canvas bag which she'd pulled out from her backpack.

"We'll help," Lila offered.

"Thanks. I guess placing these stones on the beach was pretty silly," Katherine admitted.

"Perhaps, but they did have an aesthetic quality to them," Lila commented.

Katherine stopped what she was doing to look at Lila.

"What?" Lila asked, feeling a bit uncomfortable.

"You seem to know a lot about photography," Katherine noted.

"It's my life."

Katherine gave Lila another thoughtful look before returning her attention to the shiny stones.

"Well, you've got them all," Lila stated as she stood up and handed the stones to Katherine. Good luck in your search for Bigfoot."

"I'd wish you all the best too," Katherine said. "But I don't think you'll need my blessing. You're hardly half my age but already have a brighter future in photography than I do."

"Keep following your dreams, Katherine," Lila said sincerely.

"You certainly see things through rose-colored glasses," Katherine commented with a laugh.

"No," Lila disagreed. "I see things through a 35 millimeter lens."

Lila had just turned around to leave with her friends when Katherine called, "I need your help!"

"Excuse me?" Lila asked for the second time that day.

"I need your help to find Bigfoot. Although I can't pay you, you'll get credit if we get a decent shot of the beast."

"Hold on, Katherine," Lila began. "I think you're getting too carried away. What in the world makes you think I can capture Bigfoot on camera?"

"You said you took photographs of landscapes, right?"

Lila nodded.

"Then you'll know your way around the woods," Katherine continued. "I'm not too familiar with this type of work. I usually take portraits and still-life."

"If you're not familiar with wilderness photography, why would you work on this project?" Lila demanded.

"I need the money," Katherine admitted. "The P.A.A. was the only company that would pay me a half decent wage."

"Not to mention the fame which would come with getting a photo of Bigfoot!" Pamela added.

"Pamela!" Jeannie exclaimed in shock. "Surely you don't believe in Bigfoot!"

"You're so cynical," Pamela muttered, obviously a bit embarrassed.

"You're the cynical one," Jeannie disagreed. "I'm rational."

"No one knows what the government is hiding," Pamela defended herself. "I bet they've captured all kinds of creatures. Perhaps this Bigfoot character is a surviving Neanderthal who escaped from the government's abusive treatment."

"Oh, brother," Jeannie muttered while rolling her eyes.

"Even if Lila won't help you, I will," Pamela offered.

"Are you a photographer as well?" Katherine inquired.

"No. She's a journalist," Jeannie answered for her friend.

"A journalist?" Katherine repeated with wide eyes.

"Something tells me that the P.A.A. wants their search for Bigfoot to be kept quiet," Lila noted.

Katherine looked at the sand and said quietly, "I'm getting desperate."

"Don't worry about Pamela," Lila reassured Katherine. "She won't write an article about this."

"I won't write about it, unless I get your permission," Pamela confirmed.

"Then your help will be greatly appreciated," Katherine replied thankfully. "So would yours," she added, turning to Lila.

"I...I just don't know," Lila stammered. "It seems hypocritical to be searching for something I don't believe exists."

"I felt the same way," Katherine admitted, "but that was before I saw the proof of Bigfoot's existence. I was hooked on this project as soon as I saw the photograph that an amateur photographer submitted to the P.A.A. There have been several sightings of a weird creature that stands upright and is covered in dark brown fur."

"Has The Grove Conservation Park investigated these reports?" Pamela inquired.

"I was told that the park officials roamed the area but found nothing. They abandoned their search and reasoned that either someone was playing a trick or, if there really was an animal, it had left the park grounds."

"How can you trust your source?" Pamela pressed. "There seems to be no other evidence."

Katherine sighed before answering Pamela's question. "I'll never be able to describe the image I've seen. The only way I can convince you three of Bigfoot's presence in these woods is by showing you the photograph. Would you like to see it?"

"Yes," Lila and Pamela said simultaneously.

"I guess it would be interesting," Jeannie admitted.

"Good. You'll come back to my campsite then?"

Lila, Pamela and Jeannie looked at each other quizzically. They all wondered if they should trust the woman they'd just met.

"Okay," Lila finally agreed, feeling confident that her instincts about Katherine's harmlessness were correct. "We'll come with you."

Katherine led Lila, Pamela and Jeannie through the woods and to a nearby campsite. The three friends watched as Katherine opened the door to a small car and retrieved a brown envelope.

"Gather around," Katherine instructed like a kindergarten teacher.

Lila's heart raced in excitement as she huddled close to her friends and watched Katherine reveal an eight by ten photograph from the envelope.

"This is a copy of the photograph which was taken by a camper two months ago," Katherine explained.

The photograph was in color, but it was somewhat blurry. It showed a scene of dense greenery. To the left was a tall, but thin, mammal which was covered in dark brown fur. The animal stood on its hind legs while apparently reaching for something in the bush. Unfortunately, the creature's back was to the photographer.

"What is that *thing*?" Jeannie finally managed to choke out.

"Bigfoot," Katherine said in a voice that was hardly above a whisper.

"Amazing," Pamela muttered as she studied the photograph. "Whatever it is, it's definitely not human."

"What do you think?" Katherine asked Lila.

"Well," Lila began as she peered closely at the photograph, "it doesn't look digitally altered."

"So, you think it really is Bigfoot?" Katherine pressed.

"Whatever it is, I do think it's real. You can tell that this shot was taken by an amateur. It's totally out of focus. If I was taking this photograph, I'd make sure the creature was in the center. I'd never run the risk of cutting Bigfoot out of the photograph."

"Come on, Lila, do you really think it's Bigfoot?" Jeannie demanded.

Lila didn't answer Jeannie's question. Instead, she studied every inch of the photograph.

"I've never seen an animal like this before," Lila finally spoke. "Did the P.A.A. get this photograph analyzed by a wilderness expert?"

"I suppose they would have. Whatever they did, the managers of P.A.A. can't identify this animal. Their indecisiveness led them to believe that this creature must be Bigfoot."

"This is creepy," Pamela said.

"Yeah," Jeannie agreed. "Even I don't feel safe sleeping in a tent anymore."

"If the park officials couldn't find the creature, I'm sure it's not here anymore," Pamela said aloud, more for her own comfort of mind than anyone else's. "After all, no organization, regardless of how corrupt they are, would risk the lawsuit resulting from a Bigfoot attack."

"I think we're all jumping to conclusions," Lila said rationally. Facing Katherine she said, "I'll help you search for this animal, but I can't say that I believe Bigfoot is on the loose. I'd have to see it with my own eyes to believe it."

"Thank you, Lila. Thank you all," Katherine said gratefully. "With four pairs of watchful eyes, I'm sure we'll see Bigfoot."

"We may catch Bigfoot, or whatever the creature is, if we take the appropriate actions," Lila said. "When was this Bigfoot character reportedly seen?"

"Twice at dawn and once at dusk," Katherine replied. "This particular photograph was taken at dusk."

"That would explain the photo's poor lighting. The photographer should've used a high flash," Lila said knowledgably.

"We'll just see how great your picture of Bigfoot is," Jeannie challenged. "You won't be caring about light settings with a supposedly mythical creature in front of you."

"On the contrary, dear Jeannie, I will be so professional that Bigfoot will be posing like a model for me."

"You're so realistic," Jeannie commented.

"Is there anything realistic about chasing after Bigfoot?" Pamela interrupted.

"Focus, guys," Katherine said, already acting like part of the group. "Lila is right about taking the appropriate actions. We have to search for Bigfoot at both dawn and dusk."

"And in a location which could be close to its home and feeding area," Pamela added.

"Where does Bigfoot live and feed?" Jeannie asked as she looked cautiously at the woods which surrounded them.

"I can't decipher what it's reaching for," Lila stated while looking at the photograph through squinted eyes. "Some sort of berry, I presume. Did the P.A.A. say where this shot was taken and what the photographer's subsequent action to taking the picture was?"

"No," Katherine replied. "The person who took this photo was in so much shock that she couldn't remember where the location was. After taking the picture, Bigfoot ran away. What's so interesting is that the creature hurried away in an upright position."

"So, we have no idea where this photo was taken, where Bigfoot lives or what it eats," Jeannie ticked off the number of things they didn't know on her left hand. "How in the world are we ever going to find Bigfoot?"

"The way you get any perfect shot," Lila answered dreamily. "By covering a lot of ground and then waiting for however long it takes."

That same day, Lila, Pamela and Jeannie met Katherine at her campsite before dusk. They'd parted ways since first meeting to have dinner and gather all the items they would need.

"Have you set your camera on a high flash?" Katherine asked Lila as they began to hike into the woods.

"Of course," Lila replied while smiling proudly at her high-tech camera. "I knew you were worth the extra two hundred dollars," she whispered quietly to her camera.

"We'll need to walk for roughly half an hour before reaching Little Wheat Creek," Pamela announced as she shined a small flashlight onto a map of the park.

"Why couldn't we investigate one of the other three creeks which are closer to the campsites?" Jeannie asked in a slightly nervous tone.

"The further away we are from the campsites, the more likely we are to see Bigfoot," Katherine explained.

"Perhaps," Jeannie muttered, "but our screams are less likely to be heard."

"There's no need to fear this creature," Lila commented as she shone the flashlight on the path in front of her. "There have been no reported attacks."

"As if the public would even know about it," Pamela said grudgingly.

Darkness had fallen as Lila, Pamela, Jeannie and Katherine continued walking through the dense woods. Whenever an owl hooted or someone stood on a fallen branch, they all became tense.

"This is taking forever," Jeannie complained more in fear than annoyance.

"We're almost there," Pamela said. "Let's keep going."

Jeannie hummed quietly to herself as the foursome took long strides on the path.

"Are you sure we're going in the right direction?" Lila asked suddenly.

"According to this map, we're on the right path," Pamela confirmed.

"This is hardly a path," Katherine stated while lifting her feet over a large stone which the flashlight had detected.

"Were you expecting a red carpet?" Lila joked.

"I can always dream," Katherine replied with a laugh. "Besides, you have to remember that I'm used to studios."

"Ewww!" Jeannie cried as she stepped in a warm pile of mush. "We'll, we're definitely not in a studio now," she muttered as she shone the flashlight on her dirty shoe.

"It looks like a dog has been here," Pamela commented with a wrinkled nose.

"I guess," Jeannie said as she wiped her shoe on a patch of grass. "The dog must've been here just recently because its droppings are still warm."

"It is?" Lila asked as she reached Jeannie's side. "That's weird. I haven't seen or heard a dog anywhere near here."

"Neither have I," Katherine added suspiciously. "I'm no expert but that pile looks too large to belong to a dog."

"Then what is it?" Jeannie demanded with a quivering chin.

"I'm sure it's nothing," Pamela said with a nervous laugh.

"It's probably just a bear," Katherine said confidently. "Let's keep going, guys."

"A bear!" Pamela cried.

"Relax, we don't know if it's a bear," Lila said as soothingly as she could.

"Yeah, it could be Bigfoot!" Katherine said excitedly.

As soon as the words had escaped Katherine's mouth, a loud growl sounded in the distance.

"Whatever the hell it is, I'm out of here!" Jeannie cried in terror as she turned around and ran in the direction they had come.

"Jeannie, come back!" Pamela yelled. "We have to stay together!"

Jeannie ignored Pamela as she continued to run away.

The growls became louder and fiercer. Then the sound of twigs breaking and trees rustling was heard.

"Some…something is running towards us," Pamela stuttered as she began to walk backwards.

"We better go," Katherine tried to say calmly. However, her voice was strained with fear.

"No," Lila said with determination. "I came here to photograph the creature and I won't leave until I've fulfilled my purpose."

Whether she was being brave or foolish, even Lila didn't know. She stepped forward into the oncoming sound and waited for the creature to emerge from the woods.

"Don't be an idiot," Pamela begged as she pulled on Lila's arm.

The terrifying noise became louder, but Lila still refused to move.

"We have to go," Katherine said urgently. "We have to get out of here."

A growl filled with pain and anger sounded closer to the threesome than ever before.

"Why aren't you moving?" Pamela cried as her nails buried deep into Lila's jacket. Pamela watched as Katherine fled from the area and disappeared down the dirt path.

Lila could hear the growl of the animal much clearer now. When she had first heard the noise, she wanted to grab for her camera. However, she could only stand still and listen to herself speak words of determined nonsense. Now, as the horrifying sounds grew even closer, Lila was completely demobilized. She wanted to run away but couldn't get her legs to move. It was as if she was watching life in slow motion as Bigfoot emerged from the bushes.

The creature entered the path and proceeded towards the two terrified friends. Against the darkness, Bigfoot's tall and fuzzy silhouette could be seen. The creature breathed heavily as it continued forward.

Not completely sure what she was doing, the shaken-up Pamela shone the flashlight on Bigfoot's face. The light hit the left side of its face, revealing features that were neither human nor animal. The sudden brightness startled Bigfoot, causing it to hunch over and grunt.

Taking the opportunity for survival which Bigfoot's hesitance offered, Pamela pulled Lila harder than she ever thought possible and then urged her down the path.

Still shocked but now in a more alert state, Lila ran with Pamela. The two friends breathed heavily even though they'd only been running for a few moments. Their feet pounded against the hard dirt ground so noisily that it was impossible to hear if Bigfoot was still following them.

Lila and Pamela didn't stop running until they reached Katherine's campsite. A hundred similar thoughts ran through their minds as they looked at a worried Katherine, who was pacing back and forth, and the tear-stained face of Jeannie, who was sitting anxiously in Katherine's car. The car's headlights, which were turned on to their highest beam, illuminated Katherine and the large stick she held in her hands.

When Katherine and Jeannie saw Lila and Pamela, they congregated together and then stared into the dark edge of the woods. They waited breathlessly for several minutes, but nothing emerged.

"Are...are you alright?" Katherine was the first to speak.

"I'm fine," Pamela answered through deep breaths. "Lila, are you alright?"

Although Pamela expected Lila to be shaken-up, she wasn't prepared to see such a devastated expression on her friend's face. Lila looked sadly into the woods.

"What happened back there?" Lila muttered painfully.

"We'll talk in the car," Katherine suggested.

Once they were all inside the car, the whole story of what had happened after Jeannie left came pouring out of Pamela's mouth.

"You saw it," Katherine stated. "You actually saw Bigfoot."

"We saw Bigfoot – well, Bigfoot's silhouette and half of its face," Pamela explained. "It was so weird. Bigfoot didn't look anything like I'd expected."

Pamela's heart was still racing. Although she was scared, her excitement was more powerful. *We've made an amazing discovery,* she thought deliriously.

"No one could be prepared for what happened back there," Jeannie finally spoke as she dried her eyes with a tissue. "I know I certainly wasn't. I'm so sorry for running away like that. I was just so terrified. Running away is what I do when I'm scared."

Jeannie's mind was racing with thoughts as Pamela embraced her. She thought about what Michael had done to her and how he was still in her life. Jeannie was positive that she would've stayed with Lila and Pamela if the incident with Michael had never happened. However, she also knew that she couldn't let him have a connection to her life any longer. No matter how long it took, Jeannie was determined to get Michael permanently out of her mind.

"You don't have to run anymore," Pamela whispered to Jeannie. "Lila and I know why you ran away and we forgive you."

"Of course I don't hold that against you, Jeannie," Lila added. "I wish I could've done the same." She took a deep breath before continuing. "Pamela, I have to thank you for saving me back there. If it wasn't for your quick and rational thinking, I wouldn't be here right now."

Remorsefully, Lila thought about what had just happened. Although she should've been preoccupied with the discovery of a supposedly mythical creature, she was more concerned about her own actions. Lila had always thought she was the strong one; someone who would keep calm under desperate circumstances. The contradiction of her belief, which was displayed through tonight's hysteria, disproved everything she thought she was. Lila was meant to be a superior photographer who faced any situation to get that perfect shot.

"I'm sorry for running away as well," Katherine added. "I'm the adult here, and I should've taken better care of you three. I knew what was out in these woods. I shouldn't have dragged you into this mess in the first place."

"It's not your fault," Lila said. "I was the one who misled you by claiming to be this great, fully experienced photographer."

"This self-pity thing isn't going to get us anywhere," Jeannie said suddenly. "We have to stop analyzing things and take action. We have to decide what we're going to do."

"We could tell the park officials," Lila suggested.

"Please," Katherine commented while rolling her eyes, "they weren't successful before. What makes you think they'll be any better now?"

"Katherine's right," Pamela agreed. "We've proven ourselves more capable than the park officials. I know this may sound crazy but hear me out. Although this Bigfoot creature was undeniably large, it didn't strike me as being dangerous. It seemed to be in pain. Bigfoot's face was badly hurt. I noticed a large scar on its left cheek which probably spread over its entire face. We also have to take into consideration the fact that Bigfoot didn't harm either Lila or I. And it appears that it didn't follow us back to the campsite."

"We must've stepped into its territory," Katherine added. "Bigfoot was just protecting its home."

"I want to see Bigfoot again and get my photograph." Lila felt blood pump quickly through her veins. This time, however, it pumped with desire instead of fear. Her momentary feeling of uselessness had faded. Now, her failed attempt to photograph Bigfoot only made her desire stronger.

"Are you crazy?" Jeannie cried. "I didn't see Bigfoot the first time I ventured foolishly into these woods and I certainly don't want to change that fact. We're dealing with an undiscovered, wild animal. We know nothing about it!"

"Jeannie," Pamela said slowly, while turning to face her friend. "We've made the discovery of a lifetime. Bigfoot is real, and it's our job to convince the rest of the world of its existence. It's our duty."

"You're all right," Katherine chimed in. "We've discovered something which can't go unexplored. However, we have to be careful. This is obviously a strong creature living in a delicate environment. We have to ask ourselves whether we want to uncover the mystery of Bigfoot on our own or allow someone else to do it."

"As a journalist, I have an unquenchable thirst to tell the story first," Pamela said.

"As a photographer, I must always expose the truth," Lila added.

"As a sane person, I have to request that we leave right now," Jeannie said, causing everyone to cast her a disappointed look. As she studied their faces, she knew there was no way of stopping them from fulfilling their vocations. "Fine," she snapped. "I'll help in any way I can."

"I'm glad we're all onboard," Katherine said with an appreciative smile. "The first thing we have to decide is what we want to accomplish from this. I want a few high quality shots of Bigfoot, but I don't want to cause it harm."

"My hopes are the same as yours," Lila added.

"I just want to observe Bigfoot and then write about it," Pamela said.

"I'm here for the thrill ride," Jeannie muttered sarcastically.

"Do you realize that there will be major consequences to our actions?" Katherine asked as she looked around the group of girls. "We'll either be honored for making such an incredible discovery or be scorned as lunatics who are excellent at altering photographs. If the former happens, it will be Bigfoot's life that is altered. With that said, do you still want to find Bigfoot?"

Selfishly, Lila and Pamela nodded.

Shifting uncomfortably in the car, Jeannie muttered, "I already said I would help."

"We'll stalk Bigfoot tomorrow at dawn," Katherine said. "In the meantime, let's get some sleep."

"Where are you going?" Jeannie asked in surprise as she watched Lila and Pamela exit the car.

"To our campsite," Pamela replied.

"We're going to walk in the dark?" Jeannie asked nervously as she joined them outside the car.

"Yes, but we won't be in complete darkness." Pamela switched on the flashlight she still had in her hand and smiled. "The miracle of modern technology."

"What if we run into Bigfoot again?" Jeannie asked.

"We won't see Bigfoot until tomorrow morning," Lila promised.

"Don't get too cocky," Katherine warned.

"It's called being confident," Lila defended herself as she walked into the woods, causing Jeannie and Pamela to hurry after her.

* * *

Part Five:

℘

Shattered

Lila, Pamela and Jeannie woke up early the next morning. The sun hadn't risen yet as they made their way to Katherine's campsite.

When Lila, Pamela and Jeannie reached their destination, they were greeted by a fully-prepared Katherine.

Katherine wore a typical hiking outfit which consisted of a t-shirt, shorts and lightweight boots. A camera hung securely around her neck by a thick strap.

"Ready?" Katherine asked in a whisper, even though no one else was around.

"We're ready," Lila replied quickly.

The foursome ventured away from the security of the campsite and into the woods. Katherine led the way by shining a flashlight upon the ground. Soon, the beam of light revealed a stream.

"Is this Little Wheat Creek?" Katherine whispered as she looked at the small, quickly flowing stream.

"I think so," Pamela answered quietly.

"So, where is Bigfoot?" Jeannie asked, interrupting the silence that had followed Pamela's words.

"If Bigfoot isn't going to show itself to us, we'll just have to find it," Lila stated confidently.

"Let's go upstream," Katherine suggested, leading the way once again.

By now the sun had begun to rise and was seeping through the tall trees. All that could be heard was the friend's heavy breathing and footsteps.

"I don't mean to complain," Jeannie began to say, "but how long is this creek? It seems as if we've been walking forever."

"You think everything seems like forever," Lila said. "You knew it would take a while to find Bigfoot."

"Not according to you," Jeannie spoke quickly. "Last night you wouldn't stop talking about how you'd find Bigfoot in a matter of minutes and get tons of perfect shots."

"You can't blame me for being excited," Lila pointed out.

"I don't blame you," Jeannie said through a sigh. "I just want you to get off my back."

"What does that mean?" Lila snapped.

"It means that you've changed. Ever since you got accepted into Western Heights University you've been acting like a different person."

"That is such a lie!" Lila protested while placing her hands on her hips.

"Stop it!" Pamela demanded. "We came here to find Bigfoot, not fight!"

"I'm not fighting," Lila said stubbornly.

"Of course you're not," Jeannie snapped. "You're too good to argue with me. Your personality took another major turn when this whole Bigfoot nonsense began."

"What are you talking about?" Lila demanded. "I haven't changed at all."

"Yes, you have," Jeannie argued. "You're so cocky now. Your determination to be the next great photographer is sickening."

Lila's heart raced furiously. "I'm just trying to make a career for myself, but I wouldn't expect you to understand since you have no ambitions!"

"Excuse me?" Jeannie cried in shock. "I have a lot of ambitions. I'm going..."

Jeannie never had the chance to finish her sentence as a scream sounded nearby.

"Huh?" Pamela uttered as she turned her gaze away from Lila and Jeannie. She gasped when she realized that Katherine had slipped away unnoticed.

Another terrified cry rang out in the woods. This time it was much louder.

"Come on," Pamela urged as she ran towards the noise.

Lila and Jeannie followed Pamela while looking quickly around the woods. Whether they were looking for Katherine or Bigfoot, even they didn't know.

The cries of terror became more decipherable as they turned into a plea for help.

"Help! Help me!" the voice, which was now identified as belonging to Katherine, called.

"This way!" Pamela shouted as she ran through the woods.

The noise was coming from upstream, about a hundred and fifty feet from where Lila, Pamela and Jeannie were. An angry growl came from the same location, causing the girls to stop immediately in their tracks.

"What's going on?" Jeannie moaned in between gasps of air. "Has Bigfoot hurt Katherine?"

"What the hell do you think?" Lila snapped. "She's not crying for help because a mosquito bit her."

Lila took off running; Jeannie and Pamela had to struggle to keep up. They all came to a sudden halt upon being faced with an entrance to a cave. The cave was over six feet high and four feet wide. Little Wheat Creek, which had become considerably smaller, ran into the cave.

Another shrill cry for help echoed from within the cave. Pamela was about to enter when Lila pulled her back.

"No," Lila protested. She let go of Pamela to give her a thick branch she'd found on the ground.

Pamela entered the cave with the branch held high. Lila walked beside her while shining the flashlight over the cave wall. Jeannie entered the cave, walking slowly.

"Katherine?" Lila called when the previous cries ceased to continue.

"Katherine?" Pamela joined in, calling louder than Lila.

"Help me! I'm trapped!" Katherine called back.

It was hard to tell how far away Katherine was since her voice echoed off the cave walls. Nevertheless, the threesome rushed deeper into the cave.

They came to a stop when Lila's flashlight shone against a startling scene. Bigfoot was standing upright in a corner with his face towards the cave wall. Behind Bigfoot was a horrified Katherine.

"Oh shit," Pamela muttered under her breath as she watched Bigfoot turn around and face her. She was disgusted to see what it looked like.

Bigfoot stood tall at six feet and was covered in a matted black fur. It might have been even taller if it wasn't slightly hunched over.

Pamela's eyes were drawn to Bigfoot's face. It had small beady eyes and a severely cut nose that seemed to have once been a snout. She saw a familiar-looking scar covering Bigfoot's face. Pamela also noticed that there were numerous scars all over its body. Her study of Bigfoot was cut short as it let out a furious growl and leapt towards her.

Pamela hardly had time to think as she swung the large branch in her hands at Bigfoot. The branch smacked into Bigfoot, causing it to fall to the ground.

Katherine jumped at the chance of freedom which Bigfoot's fall had provided. She scurried over its body and to Pamela's side.

"Thank you so much," Katherine gushed repeatedly.

"You can thank me later," Pamela replied. "Let's get out of here!"

The foursome hurried out of the cave and into the woods. It was sunnier now and the sudden brightness hurt their eyes, causing them to squint in response.

When Lila, Pamela, Jeannie and Katherine decided that they were a safe distance from the cave, they slowed down and tried to return their breathing to normal.

"What happened? How did you get trapped in the cave?" Lila spoke first, while glaring at Katherine.

"I decided to search for Bigfoot on my own when you and Jeannie began fighting," Katherine explained, still trying to catch her breath. "When I saw the cave, I couldn't resist the urge to explore it. I must have entered the cave when the creature was gone because when I turned around, I was face to face with it."

"That was a stupid thing to do," Lila snapped. "You should've known better than to wander off by yourself. You put us all in grave danger."

"Leave the poor woman alone," Jeannie defended Katherine. "She's just been through a traumatic experience."

"Thanks to her, so have we!" Lila yelled.

"Now is not the time to be fighting," Pamela protested. "We have to do something with that creature. We can't let it roam free."

"Why are you calling it a creature?" Jeannie inquired while trying to suppress her feelings of anger towards Lila.

"I don't think it's Bigfoot," Pamela replied. "It looked like a bear to me."

"A bear!" Lila exclaimed. "How can you say it's just a bear? Didn't you see it's face?"

"Yes, I saw it. And I got a better look at it than you did. I'm pretty sure that it's an injured bear."

"Pamela's right," Katherine finally spoke. "It's not Bigfoot."

"Oh, this is great!" Lila cried sarcastically. "You put me in danger just to photograph a deformed bear?"

"Stop it!" Jeannie shouted angrily at Lila. "You're so insensitive! Besides, if anyone is to blame, it's you."

"How the hell do you figure that?"

Lila and Jeannie's fight was interrupted by a loud rustling from a nearby bush. Everyone was silent as they watched tensely.

"What's going on here?" a man asked before stepping out from behind a large tree.

Everyone sighed in relief when they saw he was wearing a park uniform.

"Thank goodness you're here," Katherine said as she stepped towards the park official.

"A camper reported screaming coming from this area. Is everything alright?"

"No," Lila, Pamela and Jeannie replied.

"There's some sort of creature in a cave," Katherine explained. "We think it's an injured bear."

"Do you mean the cave that Little Wheat Creek runs into?" the park official inquired.

"That's the one," Katherine confirmed.

"I'll call for back-up, but first, are you all okay?"

"We're okay," Jeannie answered for everyone.

The park official took the walkie-talkie, which hung from his belt, and spoke into it. "This is Chuck. We have a situation at area one of Little Wheat Creek. I need back-up and a tranquilizer gun. There has been a sighting of a wild animal. It's categorized as being a potential threat to public safety."

"Instructions received," a voice replied from the walkie-talkie. "Back-up and a tranquilizer gun will be with you shortly."

It didn't take long for the back-up to arrive. However, it felt like an eternity as they all waited anxiously.

Lila, Pamela, Jeannie and Katherine were made to wait as Chuck, along with another park employee, entered the cave. Fifteen minutes later, Chuck and his helper emerged from the cave. They dragged the injured bear in a manner which made it look like an ill-treated teddy bear.

Lila, Pamela, Jeannie and Katherine were all embarrassed by what their Bigfoot had turned out to be.

"You've found Dandy the Dancer!" Chuck exclaimed after the bear had been placed into a cage and then into the back of the park's SUV.

"Dandy the what?" Lila asked with a lack of amusement.

"Dandy the Dancer," Chuck repeated. "It's the bear which used to perform at a local circus. When concerns about the mistreatment of Dandy were reported, the circus owner dumped the bear into the woods. He thought by doing so he'd be free of any charges. Let me tell you how wrong he was. On top of the animal abuse charges, he was imprisoned and fined for releasing a potentially dangerous animal into our park. We've had reported sightings of Dandy but have never been able to find him."

"I can't believe that," Pamela said in disgust. "Animal abuse is awful. Who could do such a thing?"

"There are some sick people out there," Chuck replied.

"What will happen to Dandy?" Jeannie asked quietly.

"Oh, Dandy the Dancer will be fine," Chuck reassured her. "I shot him with a tranquilizer. He'll be asleep for a few hours so a vet can help him."

"Would you like a ride to the park's head office?" the other park official asked.

"Yes," Lila, Pamela, Jeannie and Katherine all answered at once.

Chuck talked about The Grove Conservation Park during the ride to the headquarters. Everything he said about the park had been previously read by Lila, Pamela and Jeannie in the brochures they'd received when first entering the park.

"Here we are," Chuck said as he pulled the SUV to a stop in front of a wooden building.

"Thank you for the ride," Katherine said gratefully after exiting the vehicle.

"Thank you," Lila, Pamela and Jeannie echoed.

"No, thank you," Chuck said sincerely. "By finding Dandy the Dancer you have put my mind at ease."

No one said anything as they watched another park employee enter the SUV and then drive away with Chuck.

"Well, this has been quite an experience," Katherine said meekly.

"You can say that again," Lila muttered.

"I'm so sorry for dragging you into this mess," Katherine said sincerely. "I never imagined things would turn out how they did."

"It wasn't all done in vain," Pamela stated. "We did save Dandy the Dancer."

"I could've been working on my portfolio," Lila muttered bitterly.

"I'm sorry to have wasted your time," Katherine apologized. "I guess I better be heading back to my campsite."

Katherine disappeared into the woods, leaving Lila, Pamela and Jeannie standing by themselves.

Not a single word was spoken as Lila, Pamela and Jeannie made their way back to the campsite. Although it had been a hectic few hours, the tension was still present. Harsh words had been spoken and they couldn't be taken back.

When Lila, Pamela and Jeannie reached their tent, they stood and stared sadly at it. What looked like a happy vacation spot was now actually a symbol of bittersweet memories.

"We need to talk, Jeannie," Lila said while keeping her eyes on the tent.

Jeannie said nothing. Instead, she nodded.

"I'll make us some lunch," Pamela offered before scurrying away.

Lila walked to the folding chairs and sat down. Jeannie stood next to Lila but refused to sit down. Without saying a word, Lila stood up as well.

"I thought you were going to talk," Jeannie said in a bland tone that lacked both disdain and affection.

"I hardly know what to say," Lila admitted.

"We've known each other long enough to hear the truth from one another." Jeannie sighed before adding, "Just let it out, Lila."

"Okay, I will. I feel very hurt by what you said about my behavior. I don't see my actions as being cocky."

"That's not what it looks like to me," Jeannie replied.

"Do you really think I'm trying to annoy you?" Lila demanded.

"I wouldn't put it past you."

"Oh, come on, Jeannie. Do you really think I have the time to create a devious plan just to piss you off? I thought you knew me better than that."

Jeannie looked at Lila with large sad eyes. "In your own way, you've just told me that you don't have time for me. You've also said that we've grown apart."

"Stop analyzing everything," Lila snapped, feeling angry that Jeannie was putting words into her mouth. "You wouldn't have time to analyze every incident if you had something to work towards."

"Work towards," Jeannie repeated with a tight frown. "I suppose you mean a career?"

"Well, yes," Lila admitted.

"This is part of the problem," Jeannie pointed out. "You don't respect me because I don't have a career oriented, step-by-step plan."

"How can you accuse me of something so shallow?" Lila cried.

"It's true. Admit it, Lila, you feel superior to me." Jeannie felt her heart sink as Lila's face went red with embarrassment. Although she knew Lila felt this way about her, it still hurt to see the confession.

"I don't understand why you have no ambitions – no burning passion," Lila said.

"I'm not devoid of all feeling," Jeannie protested. "Stop making me sound like a lifeless robot."

"I'm not."

"Yes, you are."

"No, I'm not." Lila sighed. "Fighting won't resolve anything."

"It won't," Jeannie agreed.

"At least we agree on something," Lila muttered with a smirk.

Jeannie unexpectedly felt a fondness for Lila return to her heart. "Why did Michael have to do it?" she cried suddenly, more upset than ever.

A look of realization washed over Lila's face. "This isn't just about university, jobs or even my so-called cockiness – it's about a lot more. You blame me for what happened with Michael, don't you?"

"Not really. I mean I don't want to. I...I try to ignore my feelings," Jeannie stuttered.

"You know that none of this would've happened if it hadn't been for me. You can't forget far less forgive me for getting you that job in the first place."

Jeannie remained silent as she looked down.

"It goes both ways," Lila finally muttered.

Jeannie looked up in shock. "What do you mean?"

"Although Dad appeared to be cool, calm and collected after finding out what his brother did to you, it's all an act. He hasn't been the same since. This whole situation with you and Michael has really put a strain on my family."

"And you blame me for this?" Jeannie asked.

"I...I don't know," Lila stuttered. "I know I shouldn't. Logically, I know that it's not your fault."

"But somehow you can't convince your heart to feel the same."

"You speak as someone who is experiencing the same thing," Lila pointed out.

"Maybe I am."

"What are we going to do?" Lila asked after a moment of silence.

"I think the best thing to do is take a break from each other. As it stands right now, I may be annoyed with you but I still care. I couldn't bear to hate you."

"And that's where you think you're heading?"

"It's not fair to Pamela," Jeannie said, ignoring Lila's question on purpose.

"No. I suppose it's not. I'll tell her that we're leaving."

Jeannie nodded even though Lila wasn't looking at her.

Lila, Pamela and Jeannie ate lunch in silence. After that, they packed the camping supplies into the car.

Disappearing before the last item was packed, Pamela walked along the sandy beach. Feeling overpowered with emotions, she was angry that Lila and Jeannie's feud had cut their vacation short. After the turbulent morning, Pamela felt like she needed a vacation more than ever. What upset her the most, however, was the severity of Lila and Jeannie's fight. She'd never seen the emotions of anger along with apathy which, ironically, they both displayed.

Praying that the feud would blow over eventually, Pamela forced her mind to think about other things. Her thoughts traveled to the article she would write about animal abuse in the entertainment industry. She also thought about the upcoming school year. The journalism program would start in just over a month; this thought made her heart flutter with excitement. Although Pamela felt shy and a bit nervous about attending university, she had an innate feeling which told her she was ready to do this.

I have a ton of experience and natural ability, Pamela thought to herself. *I can so do this.*

Feeling more confident, as if she could handle anything, Pamela hurried back to the campsite. When she arrived at the bare campsite, she wasn't surprised to see Jeannie sitting in the car and Lila pacing back and forth in front of the woods.

"Are you ready to go?" Lila asked Pamela. Although Lila felt annoyed with Pamela's tardiness, she knew she had no right to demand an explanation.

"I'm ready."

The ride home was driven in complete silence. Pamela dropped Lila off first and helped her unload all the camping equipment.

"Thanks for everything," Lila said gratefully. "I'm sorry about cutting our camp trip short."

"Well, some things can't be helped," Pamela said.

"This seems like one of those things," Lila replied glumly.

"That's what scares me," Pamela replied in a tone that was just above a whisper.

"I better get this stuff inside," Lila said as she looked at the camping gear which littered her front lawn.

"Do you want me to help?" Pamela offered.

"No. You don't want to witness what happens when my parents ask why I'm home early." Lila sighed. "Then again, they probably knew it was coming."

"I better get back to the car," Pamela said awkwardly. "You can call me whenever you feel like it."

"I'll call you in a couple of days. Maybe we can do something – just the two of us."

"We can walk around Western Heights University together. I'm still confused by the layout."

"I'll talk to you soon." Lila gave Pamela a quick hug before turning around to face her house.

Neither Pamela nor Jeannie said anything as Pamela returned to the car and drove on.

Pamela stopped the car ten minutes later at Jeannie's house. She opened the automatic trunk door and then got out to help Jeannie carry her luggage.

"Thanks for the ride," Jeannie said meekly.

"It was no problem," Pamela lied.

"Come on. I'm sure you don't appreciate driving out of the city for less than two days of camping."

"I wish things had turned out differently, but I'm not angry."

"Too bad the same thing can't be said for Lila," Jeannie muttered.

"Things will be okay," Pamela reassured her friend. "It's just a fight."

"It's not," Jeannie protested while shaking her head. "It's much more than that. The things that have happened over the past few months have really torn us apart. And to tell you the truth, I really don't see much of a mend in our future."

"This is all Michael's fault!" Pamela cried. "Sometimes I really hate men! They do whatever they please and then leave us to live with the broken pieces. Why the hell should we suffer for their actions?"

"I know it seems unfair," Jeannie admitted. "But I can't change what's happened or my feelings about it."

"I know. Everything will be fine," Pamela soothed her friend as she embraced her.

"Yes, everything will be fine," Jeannie agreed. "But it may not be in the way which we're used to."

"Can I help carry the bags into your house?" Pamela offered after a moment of silence.

"It's alright, I can get them." Jeannie picked up her bags and walked to her front door. She stopped suddenly and turned around to ask, "We'll keep in touch, right?"

Pamela was shocked to hear her friend's words. "Of course we'll keep in touch!" she exclaimed. "You can't get rid of me that easily, Jeannie Ann Dallas."

Pamela returned to her car and watched as Jeannie entered her house and then closed the door behind her.

* * *

Part Six:

Young Love

Pamela spent the remainder of her summer vacation doing nothing profound. She spent a lot of time just sunbathing in her backyard. Pamela also saw Lila and Jeannie separately. She would take walks with Lila in local parks and then hang out at the mall with Jeannie.

Lila and Jeannie hadn't made amends. As far as Pamela knew, they hadn't even talked since the camping trip. She felt very affected by their feud. It had only been a few weeks since the break-up, but Pamela already missed spending time with both her friends.

Pamela began to think about Lila and Jeannie more as the school year loomed closer. She'd lost some of her confidence and found herself doubting all her skills.

What if I can't make any new friends? What if I'm the worst writer in all of my classes? Pamela dwelled on these negative situations. She knew she wouldn't be comforted by any thoughts or words until she actually experienced Western Heights University.

* * *

The first day of classes at Western Heights University started regardless of whether Pamela was ready or not. Although the outside of the university looked prestigious and daunting with grey walls and emblems, the interior was even more intimidating. With large classrooms and numerous students, Pamela felt lost in the crowd, especially as she settled into her first class.

"My name is Professor Hudson," a tall, graying man in his late fifties said as he walked back and forth in front of the large, brightly-lit classroom. "Welcome to Introduction to Journalism. Just as the course title indicates, I'll be teaching you the basics of journalism. Lectures will be held on Monday and Wednesday from 10:30-12:00 and will consist of me teaching theory. There will also be a tutorial once a week. Tutorials are much more personal since it splits this class of sixty into groups of twenty. I presume you have all signed up for one of the three tutorial timeslots. If you haven't, please see me after class."

Professor Hudson stopped speaking for a moment as he retrieved a thick pile of papers from his bag. "This is the course syllabus," Professor Hudson explained as he handed them out.

"I'd like to start by asking a question," Professor Hudson began once everyone had received the course syllabus. "What does journalism mean to you?"

Pamela raised her hand, confident that she had an answer which would please the professor. From the corner of her eye, she could see many students raise their hands as well. She felt her heart skip a beat as Professor Hudson pointed his finger towards her. Pamela had just opened her mouth to speak when a person from behind spoke first.

"Journalism is about telling the truth and representing the underrepresented," a guy answered.

Pamela turned around in her seat to look at the boy who had said exactly what she intended to. He wore a gray, indie rock band t-shirt and had bright blue eyes and light brown hair.

Pamela felt her heart rate increase. *He's so good-looking,* she thought.

"That's a beautiful and very insightful answer," Professor Hudson commented. "What does journalism mean to you?" he asked, looking straight at Pamela this time.

"I feel the exact same way he does," Pamela replied, responding quickly enough to make her answer sound genuine.

"Two of a kind!" Professor Hudson stated somewhat ambiguously before inquiring of another student's definition of journalism.

The class ended ninety minutes later with Professor Hudson saying he hoped everyone enjoyed their first class.

Pamela had just finished packing her pen and notebook into her backpack when she felt a tap on her shoulder. She turned around and was happy to see the boy with light brown hair smiling at her.

"Hey," he greeted. "How's my twin doing?"

"Your twin?" Pamela asked in confusion.

The boy laughed as he ran his fingers through his hair. "I was making reference to Professor Hudson's comment about us being two of a kind."

"Oh, yeah," Pamela said in realization. "That was funny," she added with a giggle. *Did I just giggle?* she asked herself in disgust.

"My name's Duncan Kellan."

"It's nice to meet you," she said while shaking the hand he offered her. "I'm Pamela Mitchell."

"That's a pretty name," Duncan commented.

There was a moment of silence that Pamela broke by asking, "So, how do you like this class so far?" She felt her cheeks redden slightly and hoped her bland question didn't bore Duncan.

"It's alright," Duncan replied. "The professor seems a bit too enthusiastic though. I mean, come on, there was no need for him to become so excited when discussing his latest article."

"I know what you mean," Pamela agreed in a whisper. "I think professors like to hear themselves talk."

Duncan laughed, which made Pamela feel more confident.

"They also use class time for shameless promotion of their work," he added with a smirk.

Pamela laughed loudly but then covered her mouth with her hands. She looked around the classroom, hoping that the professor hadn't heard what Duncan said. Pamela was surprised to see that the classroom was empty.

"Seems like we're the last ones in the class," Duncan said.

"I guess so," Pamela replied with a smile.

"Would you like to eat lunch with me?" he asked unexpectedly.

"I'd love to."

Silently, Pamela and Duncan walked through the university. Her mind raced with discussion topics but she couldn't think of one that was interesting enough to verbalize. Pamela was relieved when she finally saw the blue and red sign which read, *Cafeteria*.

"Do you need to buy your lunch?" Duncan asked as he held the door open for Pamela.

"Thanks," Pamela said as she walked through the open door. "No, I brought mine from home."

"So did I," Duncan stated. "I'm what you might call a health freak. It's also more convenient."

"I agree," Pamela said as she sat down at an empty table. "Are you studying anything other than journalism?"

"I'm doing a major in history," Duncan answered. "It's one of my other passions. I've always been interested in the history of different countries, especially Scotland."

"Are you from Scotland?" Pamela asked.

"Yes," Duncan answered proudly. "Well, my parents are. I was born here."

"I suspected you had a European background. I haven't met many Duncans."

"I've met a few Pamelas, but none were as nice as you."

Pamela's face flushed a deep shade of red. She used the opening of her lunch bag as a distraction.

"Are you studying something else as well?" Duncan inquired.

"English. I want to sharpen my writing skills as much as I can."

"Determined," Duncan stated with a small smile. "I like that."

"You have to be determined to make it in this business," Pamela pointed out. "Hell, you have to be determined just to make it into this program. I heard that over six hundred people applied but only sixty people made it."

"That's got to do wonders for one's ego," Duncan said with a laugh.

"Has it affected your ego?" Pamela asked.

"It puts a smile on my face," he admitted, "but it hasn't changed me. How about you?"

"I'm still the same person I've always been. It's too bad that other people can't handle success as well as us."

"It sounds like you're talking about someone in particular," Duncan said before he bit into his sandwich.

"I guess I am," Pamela said hesitantly.

"Go on," Duncan encouraged. "If you don't open up, you'll never get to truly know someone."

"Journalism boy speaks words of wisdom," Pamela joked.

"I'm serious, Pamela. You seem like a really cool girl who I'd like to know better."

"That's pretty presumptuous of you," Pamela said, trying to hide her embarrassment by playing with a loose thread that hung from her lunch bag.

"Perhaps, but that's the way I view this situation."

"It's my friend," Pamela said after a brief pause. "She got into the specialized photography program. Ever since finding out about her acceptance, she's become kind of snobby and cocky. Oh gosh, I hate saying these things about her. She's been my best friend for years."

"Does this girl have a name?"

"Lila."

"Well, it seems to me that Lila is suffering from a case of fifteen minutes of superiority." Noting Pamela's confused expression, Duncan continued. "It's like fifteen minutes of fame. Right now Lila is on an achievement-induced high. She's going to be cocky and self-absorbed for a little while. However, she'll soon realize that there are other students in her photography program. She'll get tired of talking about herself and regret her recent behavior. After this comes the apology and the restoration of the friend-ship."

"You could be right," Pamela said thoughtfully.

"Could be," Duncan said with a laugh.

"Now that I've opened up, it's your turn," Pamela said as seductively as she could. "What deep, dark secrets do you harbor beneath that indie rock band t-shirt?"

"I don't have any dark secrets. I guess the most complicated thing about me is my desire to write books on Scotland's history."

"That sounds intriguing, but definitely not complicated," Pamela noted.

"It's selfish of me to spend my time writing books on Scotland's history. I should be someone who makes important headlines about current news."

"Haven't you ever heard the phrase, those who don't study history are doomed to repeat it?"

"Yes," Duncan said slowly. "I don't understand what you're trying to prove though."

"I'm just saying that if we aren't informed about the past we'd repeat mistakes."

"You're very insightful," Duncan said as he studied Pamela with a smile.

Pamela and Duncan didn't say much else as they ate their lunch. The silence seemed different to her – she now felt comfortable even without saying any-thing.

"I'm home!" Pamela called as she walked into her house later that afternoon.

"Hi, Pam," Jeremy replied, emerging from the kitchen with a sandwich in his hand. "How was uni-versity?"

"Pretty good. How was your first day of middle school?" she asked her twelve-year-old brother, Jeremy.

"Great! My teacher's really cool. He loves sports and is going to coach the boys' soccer and cross-country running. I'm going to try out for both of them."

"I'm sure you'll make both teams," Pamela said affectionately as she ruffled Jeremy's hair. She smiled as she watched him pour a glass of grape juice for the two of them. Pamela had a great relationship with her brother and knew she was very lucky to have him.

Ring. Ring. Ring.

"I'll get it," Jeremy said, running to the living room to pick up the telephone. "It's Lila," he said, returning a moment later.

"Hey, Lila," Pamela greeted as she picked up the telephone. "How was your first day?"

"It was alright," Lila mumbled.

"By the sound of your voice, I get the impression that things didn't go that well."

"Nothing bad happened but the classes are so large!" Lila exclaimed unhappily.

Pamela couldn't suppress the smile that played upon her lips. She thought about what Duncan had said regarding Lila.

"I feel like a grain of sand on a vast beach," Lila said sadly. "I feel unimportant."

"That's not true," Pamela protested. "You'll always be special to your family and friends. Besides, you know you're talented."

"Thanks, Pamela, I needed to hear that. While we're on the topic of friendships, I see that you made a new friend." Lila paused for dramatic effect. "I saw you with a cute boy in the lunchroom."

"Were you spying on me?" Pamela asked in shock.

"You sound guilty," Lila said with a laugh. "Calm down, Pam. I wasn't spying on you."

"Oh," Pamela said in relief. She was glad that Lila hadn't heard the conversation she had with Duncan. "Why didn't you join us?"

"I already ate in another lunchroom. I was just passing by and didn't want to disturb you two. You seemed to be deep in conversation. What were you talking about?"

"Oh, just this and that. He's from my journalism class so we mainly talked about writing."

"What's his name?" Lila pried. "And do you like him?"

"Duncan, and we've just met!"

"So?"

"So...so it's too early to tell," Pamela finally said.

"He has potential then?" Lila asked curiously.

"Perhaps."

"Duncan must be pretty special. You haven't liked a guy for years now."

"A woman doesn't need a man," Pamela stated defensively.

"Of course she doesn't," Lila agreed. "She may, however, want one."

"Duncan is different – he's special," Pamela said almost dreamily.

"Pamela's in love!"

"No, I'm just in like."

"In like for now," Lila said suggestively.

"What about you?" Pamela asked, hoping that changing the topic would reduce the redness of her face. "Have you met anyone nice?"

"No. I feel shy towards the other students in my class," Lila admitted.

"I'm sure it'll pass."

"I hope so. I think my shyness stems from never having to be alone. I've always been with you and Jeannie. I had no need for more friends." Lila paused for a moment. "How is Jeannie?" she inquired quietly.

"Jeannie is doing well. She recently got a job as a receptionist."

"A receptionist at what company?" Lila asked.

"It's a not-for-profit thing."

"And this service is?" Lila asked, getting annoyed at Pamela's lack of willingness to tell her.

"It's a women's help center."

Lila fell silent. She suddenly understood the reason for Pamela's reluctance. "Good for her," she finally said. "I have to go now and help Dad cook dinner. Maybe I'll see you tomorrow at school."

"See you later, Lila," Pamela said before hanging up the telephone.

* * *

"Hey, Duncan, I thought you were in the afternoon tutorial?" Pamela asked in surprise as she saw him waiting outside the journalism classroom the next morning. It was only the second day of school but she was already feeling more confident and capable.

"I switched my timetable," Duncan said with a casual shrug.

Pamela didn't say anything as they entered the classroom. She wanted to believe that he'd changed his tutorial timeslot for her.

"Welcome to the first tutorial for Introduction to Journalism," Professor Hudson greeted once everyone was seated. "Today I will be teaching you the basics of conducting interviews."

Pamela listened as Professor Hudson discussed the finer points of interviewing.

"For your first assignment," Professor Hudson said sixty minutes later, "I'd like you to partner with someone."

"Will you be my partner?" Duncan whispered to Pamela.

"Of course," she whispered back.

"Both partners will be required to interview each other. As the interviewee, you will pretend to be someone who's in the public eye. For example, you could pretend to be a politician, actor, movie director or a professor. There aren't many rules to this project except that both partners must play the role of the interviewer and interviewee. When being interviewed, each partner must pretend to have a different career. What I mean by this is that you both can't be interviewed as an actor, you must choose different characters. Needless to say, this assignment should be taken seriously and treated in a professional manner. The typed, double-spaced, three page interviews are due at the beginning of class next week. I wish you all success in this assignment. It will count for five percent of your final grade."

"I guess we should get started on this assignment right away," Duncan said as he walked out of the classroom with Pamela. "Do you know what public figure you want to play?"

"I want to be a journalist," Pamela answered.

"We both have to play the interviewer and interviewee, remember?"

"I know. I just think it would be cool for a professional journalist to be interviewed. I could talk about doing fieldwork and stuff like that."

"That actually sounds really cool," Duncan agreed. "I bet no one else will be doing that."

"I hope not. So, what type of public figure do you want to be?" Pamela asked.

"A politician. Hell, if the whole concept of politics wasn't so corrupt, I'd run for office in reality."

"Sounds intriguing," Pamela commented. "I only have one other class today so I'll be done by 12:30."

"I'm done at one o'clock. Do you want to meet at the library then?"

"The library is always packed by noon," Pamela pointed out. "Perhaps we could work at my house. It would be much quieter there and it's only a ten minute bus ride away."

"I have my car. I could drive us, if you like," Duncan offered.

"Sounds good. I better get to class now. I'll see you outside the journalism classroom, right?"

"I'll be there. Later, Pamela."

"Bye, Duncan," Pamela said before hurrying down the hall. *I think this might be my favorite school assignment ever,* she thought with butterflies in her stomach.

"Hey, Pamela, are you ready to go?" Duncan asked as he approached her outside the journalism classroom.

"I'm all set," she replied, noting that he wasn't only cute but also punctual.

Pamela and Duncan talked about their assignment while walking towards the university's parking lot.

"This can't be your ride!" Pamela exclaimed when Duncan stopped next to a large red pick-up truck.

"It's a hybrid," Duncan said proudly.

"Sweet chrome job," Pamela said as Duncan opened the door for her. "Your parents must really love you," she teased.

"I'm a lovable guy," Duncan said with a wink.

Five minutes later, Pamela and Duncan arrived at the Mitchell's house.

"Come in," Pamela said politely, after unlocking the door.

"Nice house," Duncan commented while looking around.

"Thanks. My mom's an interior designer." Pamela then added, "Can I get you anything to eat or drink?"

"I'm okay – thanks."

"We should get started on our project then," Pamela said, leading him up to her bedroom.

"Nice room," Duncan commented a moment later as he saw the walls covered with autographed indie rock band posters.

"You're full of compliments today," Pamela noted with a laugh.

"I always speak the truth," Duncan said, facing Pamela. "Do you want me to interview you first?"

"No. I'll interview you."

"Fire away," Duncan challenged as he sat on Pamela's unmade bed.

"Sorry for the mess," she apologized. "I've just been so busy lately."

"I don't mind," Duncan said, obviously comfortable in his surroundings.

"Okay, Mr. Politician," Pamela began as she sat opposite Duncan on the bed. "Please state your name and the position you're running for."

"My name is Duncan Kellan and I'm running for the position of President."

"As a Presidential candidate, what promises are you making to the voting public?"

"I don't believe that our society needs a radical change. Instead, it needs to mend its imperfections."

"What do you consider the imperfections of our society to be?" Pamela grilled.

"Violence, homelessness and lack of jobs as well as government funded programs."

"How would you curb violence?"

"I don't want to just curb violence. I want to banish it completely."

"That sounds like a very difficult task, Mr. Kellan. How do you propose to fulfill this goal?"

"By implementing harsh punishments to those who engage in acts of violence."

"Are you suggesting that our society bring back capital punishment?"

"Not at all! The harsh punishments would include longer prison sentences, steep fines and numerous hours of laborious community service. I think life in prison is much harsher than death."

"How would you deal with homelessness?"

"The issues of homelessness and the lack of jobs as well as government funded programs are closely related. I think we need to place a great deal of time and money into education centers and daycare facilities."

"Your ideas sound very utopian," Pamela noted. "Who would be paying for these services?"

"The money would mainly be derived from taxes and better budgeting."

"That won't please the majority of voters."

"Perhaps not, but I foresee the benefits out-weighing the drawbacks in the near future. Society wins when its citizens are employable and self-sufficient."

"That's one of the most honest and humane things I've ever heard a politician say," Pamela muttered, almost forgetting that she was meant to be a professional journalist.

"Things don't have to stay the same. They can change for the better," Duncan stated as he came closer to her.

Pamela felt her heart rate increase. She was overcome with fondness and passion. Duncan wasn't only very attractive, he was also the most prolific thinker she'd ever met.

Duncan's perfect for me, she thought as she leaned in closer and kissed him.

The kiss was sweet and exciting. The longer it lasted, the more passionate it became.

"I need to breathe," Duncan said lightheartedly as he pulled away from Pamela a few minutes later.

Pamela looked at him with wide eyes and then jumped off the bed.

"Oh my gosh," she muttered. "I'm so sorry. I can't believe I just did that."

"Hey, wait a minute," Duncan said gently. "There's nothing to regret or be ashamed of."

"I've never been so bold."

"Well, I'm glad you made an exception for me." Duncan pulled Pamela closer and kissed her.

"I'm not the kind of girl who believes in love at first sight," Pamela stated after their lips had parted. "I don't believe you can know someone just by looking at them or that you'll experience flying sparks with one passing gaze."

"This doesn't sound too optimistic," Duncan said with a nervous laugh.

"I don't believe in these things but you sure as hell brought me close to accepting them as true." Pamela paused to lay her eyes intently upon Duncan's. "What I know for certain is that you're a really special guy who thinks the same way as I do. I can't think of anything else I'd rather do than get to know you better."

"Your feelings don't go unrequited," Duncan reassured her. "You're beautiful and your personality intrigues me – that's something which no girl has ever been able to accomplish before."

"We *are* a good match," Pamela confirmed with a laugh. "I don't think anyone else would express their feelings in such an eloquent way. They're more likely to say, you're hot – want to be my boyfriend?"

"I can execute my words to suit the norms of modern language. You're hot, Pamela. Want to be my girlfriend?"

"Yes," Pamela replied with a laugh as she embraced Duncan and kissed him. Her whole body shivered as he placed his hands on her waist.

"What the hell is going on?" a loud voice interrupted.

Pamela jumped away from Duncan and almost fell over the clothes which lay on her bedroom floor.

"Mom!" Pamela gasped.

Mrs. Mitchell's eyes scanned the bedroom. She looked at the boy she'd never seen before and the sheet-tangled bed. Mostly, however, Mrs. Mitchell looked at her guilt-ridden daughter.

"Who is he?" Mrs. Mitchell finally choked out.

"Um, this is Duncan. He's from my journalism class."

"Hi," Duncan said meekly while avoiding eye contact with Pamela's mother.

"So, you've known Duncan for two days then," Mrs. Mitchell stated as she crossed her arms and looked disapprovingly upon the scene.

"Yes," Pamela replied in a weak voice.

"We were working on our journalism project," Duncan began to explain.

"This is quite a project," Mrs. Mitchell interrupted.

"We *were* doing our work," Duncan said firmly as he picked up his backpack from Pamela's bed. "I better get going now. I'll see you at school tomorrow, Pamela. It was nice meeting you, Mrs. Mitchell. I'll show myself out."

Pamela watched as the blabbering Duncan exited her bedroom. She hoped that this incident hadn't scared him away or changed his opinion of her. Her mind quickly turned to more dire issues as she saw her mother's stern expression.

"What are you doing home from work?" Pamela asked the worst question possible.

"You planned this?" Mrs. Mitchell cried with wide eyes.

"No! It's not what you think. Duncan and I were just doing our homework."

"Do you take me for a fool?"

"Of course not!" Pamela cried. "It was just a kiss."

"It looked like more than just a kiss," Mrs. Mitchell replied, raising her eyebrows at the messy bed.

"Oh, get real," Pamela mumbled in embarrassment. "You saw everything that happened. Here, look at my notes. They contain all the work we did since arriving here."

Mrs. Mitchell looked at the notebook which Pamela handed to her. It contained several pages of scribbled notes.

"Do you always do homework in bed?" Mrs. Mitchell demanded, trying desperately to gain the truth of what really happened.

"I only have one chair," Pamela pointed out, "and it's covered with clothing. I forgot to make my bed this morning, that's all."

Mrs. Mitchell looked around the messy bedroom, finally convinced that Pamela was telling the truth. "I have to get back to work. I only came home to get some paperwork I left in the den. Now I wish I hadn't."

"Mom, nothing happened."

"I know, but I still want to discuss some things with you tonight."

Pamela experienced an array of emotions as she watched her mother leave. She was embarrassed that she'd been caught kissing a boy. However, she was also embarrassed that Duncan had witnessed the incident with her mother. Pamela felt angry that her special moment with Duncan had been interrupted. It was as if her mother was suppressing her from growing up and withholding a right she ought to have.

"I'm so confused," Pamela muttered as she fell onto her bed.

* * *

Pamela was nervous about seeing Duncan. It was just yesterday that the embarrassing incident at her house had occurred. Now, as she walked up the university's noisy hallway, she wondered how he'd react. Her curiosity was short-lived as she saw him waiting outside the journalism classroom for her.

"Hey," Duncan greeted shyly. "Is everything alright between you and your mother?"

"Things are a bit awkward," Pamela confessed, "but she knows that nothing happened."

"Good," Duncan said through a sigh of relief. "I'm afraid I haven't made a good first impression though."

"So, we're okay?" Pamela asked nervously.

"Of course we're okay. Although the events of yesterday were a 10.0 on the Richter scale of embarrassment, I have more important things to worry about."

"Such as?" Pamela pried.

"Such as getting to know you better and finishing our project," Duncan replied with a wide smile.

"Right, the project – I almost forgot. I don't think it's a good idea to finish it at my house," Pamela said while thinking about the talk she had with her mother last night. "We'll have to work in the library."

"I thought you said the library is too busy." Duncan suddenly sighed. "I'm sorry, Pamela. I'm just being difficult. I can understand why you don't want me to come to your house."

"It's not that *I* don't want you to come," Pamela explained. "It's my mother. She doesn't think it's a good idea for us to be alone."

"Why do I suddenly feel like a savage dog?"

"Oh, Duncan, please don't take this personally. My mother is overprotective when it comes to things like this."

"I understand," Duncan said reassuringly as he placed his hand gently on her shoulder. "Really, I do. It may comfort you as well as your mother to know that I'm old-fashioned, if you know what I mean."

"I'll be sure to let my mother know that," Pamela said with a smile as she led Duncan into the classroom.

* * *

Part Seven:

℘

The Complex

The months flew by as Pamela busied herself with schoolwork. She was doing well in all her courses, achieving high marks that were above the class average. Although Pamela studied hard, she made time for Duncan and her friends. She usually saw Duncan outside of class and had fun getting to know him better. He even came to her house regularly. All the embarrassment from Mrs. Mitchell and Duncan's first meeting had dissolved. Things were going extremely well with him. The more Pamela learned about Duncan, the more she liked him.

Lila was doing well in school and had accepted the fact that there were other people at Western Heights University who had talent. She'd even lost some of her shyness and had made a few friends who were also in the photography program.

Jeannie had worked her way up to co-supervisor of the women's help center due to her dedication and hard work. However, she still worked one-on-one with the women who needed help. Jeannie had even been presented with an award for all the great work she did at the center.

Pamela missed hanging out with Lila and Jeannie at the same time, but she was grateful for maintaining such a strong bond with each friend.

* * *

There was only one month left in the school year and the pressure to meet deadlines and prepare for exams was looming.

"It's time for your final assignment," Professor Hudson stated as he walked back and forth in front of the large classroom. "I'm passing around a piece of paper which has a detailed description of how this assignment will work."

"Oh, this is great!" Pamela said enthusiastically as she read the description of the assignment.

"What is it?" Duncan asked.

"Sorry," she muttered, finally realizing that she was still holding the bundle of papers.

"Whoa!" Duncan exclaimed with wide eyes after reading the description of the assignment. "We're going to do fieldwork!"

"It says here that we have to make a consultation with Professor Hudson to receive our topic." Pamela smiled as she thought about the extremely important topic she'd be assigned to cover.

Pamela and Duncan went to see Professor Hudson right after class. Duncan had the first consultation. He emerged from the professor's office a few moments later with a big smile on his face.

"What are you reporting on?" Pamela asked.

"I'll be covering the platform of a political party for a whole week!" Duncan said excitedly.

"That's great!" Pamela exclaimed, happy to hear that Professor Hudson had chosen appropriate topics for his students.

Duncan watched Pamela enter Professor Hudson's office. He was surprised to see her exit the office a few minutes later with a sour expression on her face.

"You won't believe what topic Professor Hudson chose for my assignment!" Pamela cried.

"If I won't believe it, I definitely won't be able to guess," Duncan pointed out. "Tell me."

"Hayden Stevenson!"

"Huh?"

"I have to write an article about Hayden Stevenson!" Pamela cringed just thinking about her assignment.

"I heard you the first time," Duncan stated with furrowed eyebrows. "I still don't understand though. Isn't Hayden a child actor from that new television show?"

"Yeah, he plays Jesse on *Victorious.*"

"So, what are you reporting on? I'm still confused," Duncan confessed.

"So am I," Pamela said. "Why would Professor Hudson assign me such a superficial topic? He wants me to job-shadow Hayden on the set of *Victorious* for a week and then write an article about him as well as my experience there."

"Well, now that you've explained the assignment, it doesn't sound that bad. In fact, I bet many people would love to visit the set and meet Hayden. *Victorious* is a pretty popular show, after all."

"I don't care about the entertainment industry! I want to report on something important. Professor Hudson must think I'm a horrible writer. Why else would he assign me such an inane topic?"

"Calm down," Duncan said soothingly as he placed his arm around her. "I'm sure Professor Hudson knows that you're a very competent writer. Perhaps he even thought he was doing you a favor. You'll be able to sell your article on Hayden to a magazine publisher as well as get school credit for it."

"I know you're trying to make me feel better, but it's not working. I have to go to my other class now. I'll see you later." Pamela hurried down the hall and towards her next class. All she could think about was her assignment which had no merit.

* * *

Pamela's work on her journalism assignment began the following Monday. She exited the noisy, crowded subway and headed in the direction of Shining Star Studios.

Pamela was still angry at Professor Hudson for making her report on such a frivolous topic. She kept Duncan's comment about selling the article to a magazine in the forefront of her mind. Regardless of how she felt about the assignment, Pamela knew a publisher would pay good money to get an inside scoop on the television show. She also knew that having an article published in a major magazine would look fantastic on her CV. Pamela decided to ignore her anger towards Professor Hudson and concentrate on the task at hand. She'd even done homework on Hayden's career as well as watching several episodes of *Victorious*. Although she'd seen the television show before, Pamela had never been a fan.

Victorious was about a single mother who juggled a full-time job while keeping the house in order and raising two children. One of these children, played by Hayden, was an aspiring track runner who usually got into trouble. In Pamela's opinion, *Victorious* was a semi-clichéd television show which offered cheesy moral lessons at the end of each episode. The one thing Pamela did like about the television show, however, was the way it portrayed the struggles of being a single mother.

"Sorry," Pamela muttered as she bumped into a person who was walking in the other direction. She quickened her pace and hurried along the street.

This part of the city is always busy, she thought while looking at the tall buildings which made up the entertainment district.

When Pamela finally arrived at Shining Star Studios, she gained access to the building by showing the security guard the identification card she had received from Professor Hudson. She was then guided down the red carpeted hall by an employee and directed to wait in a room which was filled with electrical wires and unplugged spotlights.

"Jimmy, the university student is here!" the employee, who had escorted Pamela, called before turning around and disappearing through the large gray doors.

"You must be Ms. Pamela Mitchell!" Jimmy exclaimed as he came from an adjacent room.

"Yes," she said politely while shaking his hand.

"I'm the creator and director of *Victorious*," Jimmy introduced himself. "I'm glad you could make it."

"Thanks for having me."

"We have a full day ahead of us. We'll be filming in studio B2 which is right over there." Jimmy stopped talking to turn around and point to the studio he'd just come from. "The episode we're currently shooting deals a lot with Mimi Streets. She plays Jesse's mother."

"I know," Pamela replied with a friendly smile.

"Hayden will be coming into the studio in an hour or so. In the meantime, you can watch the scenes with Mimi."

Pamela allowed Jimmy to guide her towards the set. She was astonished to see how many people were there. Several crew members were positioning large spotlights, adding final touches to the living room set, doing hair and make-up, checking the electrical wiring and performing many other tasks. Her senses were fully alert as she watched the hurried movements of the cast and crew. Against her own will, she was having fun.

Pamela watched as Mimi entered the set along with a handsome older man. Bright lights from overhead suddenly shined on the living room set. As Pamela shielded her eyes, she unexpectedly gained an appreciation for actors. She knew there was no way she could perform under such conditions.

"Actors in position, please!" Jimmy called. "And action!"

"You better leave," Mimi, as Ms. Darlington, said so loudly and clearly that Pamela jumped in surprise.

"Is that what you really want?" the man, who played a character Pamela was unfamiliar with, asked. "Or is it just what you think you should want?"

"I don't have time for psychoanalysis," Ms. Darlington replied as she hurried to pick up a set of keys which lay on a nearby table.

"And I don't have time for games," the man said quietly as he opened a door on the set and walked solemnly through it.

Pamela watched carefully as Mimi used only facial expressions to convincingly portray a woman in distress.

"And cut!" Jimmy yelled so loudly that Pamela jumped once again.

"I could have acted better in my sleep," a small voice snickered from behind Pamela.

Pamela turned around to see a young boy with curly blonde hair and green eyes. She instantly recognized him as Hayden Stevenson.

"You must be the lucky student who gets to job-shadow me," Hayden said while looking Pamela up and down.

"Um, yes. My name's Pamela Mitchell," she said, very taken aback by Hayden's rude tone.

"I don't need to know your name," Hayden snapped. "You're the one interviewing me, remember?"

"I...I know that."

"Do you have a stutter or something? If you do, maybe the interview would be more successful if you just wrote the questions down."

Pamela's mouth fell open in shock. *How can someone who looks so angelic be so mean?* she thought while watching Hayden's blonde curls bounce up and down as he approached the director.

"I'm ready for my scene," Hayden demanded.

"Alright, Mr. Stevenson," Jimmy replied while hurrying to prepare for Hayden's scene.

Pamela was flabbergasted by Jimmy's reaction to Hayden's demand. *No wonder Hayden is so spoiled,* she thought. *When people give in to his demands, they're reinforcing his bad behavior.*

"Your article better make me look good," Hayden threatened.

"How could I possibly make you look bad?" Pamela said, trying to suppress her sarcasm.

"If you mess things up for me, you'll be really sorry."

"I wouldn't dream of it," Pamela said through clenched teeth.

"We're ready to begin the scene," Jimmy informed Hayden.

"It took you long enough," Hayden snapped before heading towards the set.

Pamela was amazed to see such a transformation in Hayden's behavior when Jimmy yelled, "Action!" He'd gone from a spoiled brat to a sensitive son in a matter of seconds.

"I guess that's why they call it acting," Pamela said to herself in a voice that was just above a whisper.

"That was some fine acting," Pamela complimented sincerely as Hayden exited the set. She shot him a smile, hoping to add a hint of friendliness.

"Of course it was," Hayden responded. "I'm the best actor there is."

Pamela was stunned by how Hayden's rude behavior failed to faze him. Pamela knew she'd never be able to act like that and then walk away unaffected.

"Are you going to be following me all day?" Hayden demanded unhappily.

"Yes, it's my job."

"I wish I hadn't agreed to do this job-shadowing thing," Hayden stated as he walked into his dressing room and then slammed the door in Pamela's face.

I wish you had refused as well, Pamela thought while staring at her watch. *Three hours down. Only one more week to go.*

"How was your first day on set?" Duncan asked Pamela after she'd picked up the ringing telephone in her living room.

"Apart from having to deal with a spoiled brat who will go unnamed, it was actually pretty cool," Pamela said as she sat down on the faux leather sofa.

"So much preparation goes into television production."

"I suppose Hayden isn't as sweet as he looks?" Duncan asked with a laugh.

"He's so rude to everyone – including the director. He's also unbelievably demanding. At least some good came from meeting him."

"What's that?"

"It makes me appreciate my brother more than ever!" Pamela exclaimed. "What would I do if I had to live with someone like Hayden?"

"Move out," Duncan replied.

"That would probably be my only option," Pamela laughed. "Let's not talk about Hayden. Tell me how your day was."

"It was amazing!" Duncan answered enthusiastically. "I went all over the city to attend the different conferences that the political leader was speaking at. He has some really good ideas. He sure has my vote!"

"I'm glad you had a good day," Pamela said sincerely. "I have to go now. My dad's telling me to come to the table before dinner gets cold."

"Alright, Pamela, I'll talk to you tomorrow – if you survive the wrath of Hayden!"

"Very funny," Pamela muttered before hanging up the telephone.

* * *

The next morning, Pamela left her house extra early. She wanted to beat the morning rush and perhaps spend a bit more time with Jimmy. For someone whose career fell into the category of what she used to consider superficial, she had a surprising amount of respect for him.

It was a warm day and Pamela was grateful to get outside, even if it was only in the city. As she neared Shining Star Studios, she was shocked to see two police cars in the parking lot.

"If you receive any information, please be sure to contact us," Pamela heard one of the police officers say to Jimmy.

"Of course," Jimmy replied while looking very serious.

Pamela stood still as she watched the police officers enter their cars and drive away.

"Pamela!" Jimmy cried when he saw her standing there. "Something awful has happened! You better come inside."

Pamela followed Jimmy over the red carpet floors until they reached studio B2.

"What's going on?" Pamela demanded as Jimmy came to a stop and then threw himself onto the director's chair.

"It's just awful! Hayden has disappeared!"

Pamela's heart rate increased rapidly. "What do you mean he's disappeared? People don't just vanish into thin air!"

"Well, apparently Hayden Stevenson has."

"You can't dump this information on me without giving me all the facts. When was Hayden last seen? When was it realized that he was missing?"

"The police began their investigation just a couple of hours ago," Jimmy answered. "When Mrs. Stevenson went to wake up Hayden this morning, she discovered that his bed was empty. She searched their house and neighborhood, but she couldn't find him."

"It wasn't a kidnapping, was it?" Pamela asked with a heavy heart and a lump in her throat.

"There has been no reason to treat Hayden's disappearance as a kidnapping," Jimmy replied. "However, due to his status, it may be a possibility."

"Oh, poor kid," Pamela muttered unhappily. "Wherever Hayden is, he must be so scared. And his poor mother – she must be going out of her mind with worry."

"We're all going mad with worry," Mimi said with a sigh, seemingly appearing out of nowhere.

Pamela cast Mimi a sympathetic gaze when she saw her tear-stained face.

"Nothing good can come out of this," Mimi stated with a sudden outburst of anger. "You hear stories about kids like Hayden being kidnapped and held for ransom."

"But Jimmy said there was no reason to treat Hayden's disappearance as a kidnapping," Pamela reminded her.

"And so we shouldn't," Jimmy interrupted.

"What do you think happened then?" Mimi demanded with her hands on her hips.

"We've all had a rough morning," Jimmy commented while avoiding Mimi's question. "We might as well go home. I can't shoot any scenes without Hayden anyway."

Pamela nodded numbly. "Please let me know if you hear anything," she requested before leaving studio B2.

As Pamela walked down the hall, she thought about what had just happened.

It wasn't until she reached the subway that Pamela began to get suspicious. She thought about how Jimmy had avoided Mimi's question regarding the cause of Hayden's disappearance. *Perhaps Jimmy kidnapped Hayden,* Pamela thought as she stepped onto the subway. *Jimmy will lay low for a couple of days and then demand a large ransom for Hayden's safe return. Or perhaps Jimmy kidnapped Hayden because he was sick of being bullied by him.*

By the time Pamela had reached her home, her mind was swimming with suspicions and what-if scenarios.

"Having journalistic instincts can suck sometimes," Pamela muttered as she entered her house. She'd decided that she didn't have enough evidence to prove that Jimmy was somehow connected to Hayden's disappearance.

The empty house made Pamela feel eerie. After today's events, she wished someone could be with her.

Pamela headed to her bedroom, determined to complete some English homework. As usual, her bedroom was a mess. Clothing littered the floor and her English books lay at the foot of her bed.

Pamela jumped onto her bed and began to read a novel she had to write an essay on. She was completely engrossed in the book until she heard something creak. Unsure of what had caused the noise, she ignored it and used rational thinking to blame it on a tree branch which was probably scraping against the window.

"I can't concentrate anymore," Pamela complained aloud an hour later. "I might as well do something else." The sound of her own voice comforted her. She still felt uncomfortable and wanted desperately to invite a friend over. Unfortunately, Duncan was busy with his journalism assignment, while Lila was at school and Jeannie was at work.

Pamela had just risen from her bed when the creak sounded again. She stood still and listened. The noise came again, this time much louder. Pamela's heart began to race when she realized that the noise was coming from her closet.

Each of Pamela's legs felt as if they weighed a hundred pounds, but somehow she urged herself to the closet door. The noises had stopped. It was as if whoever – or whatever – was behind the door had ceased to stir.

The golden doorknob felt unusually cold in Pamela's hand as she grasped it tightly. Ignoring her instincts which told her to run, she flung the door open. Her eyes went wide and her mouth hung open when she saw who was in her closet.

"Hayden!" Pamela exclaimed. "What are you doing here?"

Hayden, who was hugging his knees to his chest, looked up slowly.

Pamela saw something in Hayden's eyes which she never thought he was capable of expressing; he looked frightened and uncertain.

"What are you doing here?" she demanded when he failed to offer a response.

"I had to get away!" Hayden cried while emerging from Pamela's closet.

"Why?" Pamela asked in a gentler tone.

"Don't try to be nice to me," Hayden snapped as he walked around her bedroom as if he owned it.

"Drop the tough act, Hayden. Don't you know how scared everyone is?"

"That's a lie!" Hayden said with so much hatred that Pamela was taken aback.

"It's not a lie," Pamela said firmly. "Everyone is really concerned. Do you realize that the police are looking for you?"

"I don't care," Hayden said with a shrug.

Pamela saw the flicker of fear which passed in Hayden's eyes. She said nothing as she looked at him.

"Stop looking at me," Hayden commanded.

"If I don't look at you, will you tell me what's going on?" Pamela bargained.

"You're crazy."

"With all due respect, I'm not the one hiding in a stranger's closet." Pamela sighed when Hayden remained silent. "Sit on the floor with your back to me," she instructed as she sat on the floor.

Hayden sighed but sat on the floor with his back to Pamela anyway. "Let's get this over with as fast as possible."

"Why did you run away from home?" Pamela questioned.

"Who said I ran?" Hayden snapped. "Maybe you kidnapped me."

"We both know that's not true. Why did you run away, Hayden?"

"What do you want me to say? I bet you want me to confess that my work has become too much for me and that I'm overwhelmed. You also want me to say I just want to be a normal kid, don't you?"

"I only want you to say it if it's true."

"Then I'm saying it!" Hayden exclaimed unexpectedly. "All of this is too much for me. You have no clue what being a child actor is like."

"You're right," Pamela agreed. "Tell me about it."

"It's awful! I have to work longer hours than my own father! And there's so much pressure. My mistakes don't just affect me and upset my parents, they cost hundreds of dollars for the producers of whatever project I'm working on."

"You're just a kid, Hayden. No amount of talent will change that fact."

"Talent may not change that fact but the years certainly can."

"What do you mean?"

"I mean that I'm getting older. I'm twelve – that horrid age which comes before the neither nor period." Seeing Pamela's confused expression, he continued. "They're the years which I am neither cute nor handsome. Soon, I'll be another face in the *Whatever Happened To* column."

"Didn't you just tell me that you *wanted* to be a normal kid?"

"I don't know what being a normal kid is. I can work up to fourteen hours a day and then be so tired that I can't stay awake for the drive home. Things aren't much better when I have the occasional day off. When I'm not working, my body is in the mode to do something. I can't sit still. I don't know what I want, Pamela, I just don't know."

"I know what your family, friends and the police want," Pamela said after a few moments of silence. "They want to know that you're safe."

"Please don't call my mother," Hayden begged as Pamela stood up and reached for the telephone. "If you have to call someone, call the police."

"Excuse me?" Pamela asked with shock. "You would rather I call the police than your own mother?"

"That's what I said."

"You know that the police don't look kindly upon people who waste their time, right?"

"But I'm a star."

"Do you really think the police care what your profession is?"

"They obviously do if they're looking for me," Hayden said smugly while crossing his arms. "I thought police only take a missing person report seriously after twenty four hours have passed."

"You know you're smart, Hayden, and so do I. Just go home. Don't put yourself, along with everyone else, through this."

"I can't! I'll be in so much trouble!"

"Do what you have to do, Hayden. Do it and then deal with it. You can't run forever."

Hayden looked up at Pamela in defeat. "If I go back home, things will just be the same. I don't want to deal with so much pressure."

"Then don't. Tell your mother how you feel."

"I've never done that before."

"Then I think it's time you learned how." Pamela cast Hayden a sympathetic glance before lifting up the telephone.

Pamela stood outside her house with Hayden as they waited for Mrs. Stevenson and the police to arrive.

"Are you going to be alright?" Pamela inquired, seeing the police car approaching them.

"Maybe." Hayden looked down at the ground in embarrassment. However, when he lifted his head, he was smiling. "Since you helped me, I'd like to return the favor."

"How can you help me?" Pamela asked in confusion.

"By giving you advice on where *not* to hide the key to your house. Seriously, Pamela, finding your home address in Jimmy's desk, which he always leaves unlocked, wasn't as easy as figuring out that you kept a spare key under the front door mat. Find a better hiding place," Hayden added as he flung the key to her and then hurried to his mother's side.

Pamela watched in awe as the police and Mrs. Stevenson surrounded Hayden in concern.

"I have a feeling that he'll be alright," Pamela whispered to herself.

* * *

Pamela's instincts about Hayden were correct. The shooting of *Victorious* resumed two days later with a promise that its child star would be given fewer responsibilities. Although Hayden still wanted to act, he and his mother had come to the understanding that he could be a kid first.

Pamela's article about her experience of job-shadowing Hayden was very different from what Professor Hudson had expected. She focused her article on the rewards, as well as hardships, of being a child actor. Pamela received an "A" on the project and had it published in a serious career magazine. She knew she would've made more money by writing an article specifically about *Victorious*, but that no longer mattered. Pamela felt ashamed that she'd ever thought about selling out to a writing market which she loathed. Now, more than ever, Pamela understood the power which came with the written word.

* * *

Part Eight:

℘

Unbroken

Exam week, which marked the end of Pamela's first year at university, came and then went. She was exhausted by all the hard work she'd done and was ready for summer vacation. However, Pamela managed to muster up enough energy for one final project. This project would be the most important assignment she'd ever done because it could possibly bring Lila and Jeannie back together. Although Pamela had wanted to reunite her two estranged friends since the break-up, she hadn't had the courage to do so. She'd been too afraid to try since a failure on her part could lead to disastrous results. However, Pamela's relationship with Duncan and the whole experience with Hayden had given her a new outlook on humanity. She now believed that people could grow, forgive and be unselfish.

"Is this the last picture?" Duncan asked as he taped a photograph onto Pamela's bedroom wall.

"Yes, that's them all," Pamela replied as she stood back to look at all the hard work they had done.

Pamela's bedroom had been thoroughly cleaned and decorated for a small party which was to take place in a matter of minutes. The decorations, which were photographs of Pamela, Lila and Jeannie, covered her bedroom wall.

"I better go before they arrive," Duncan said.

"Thank you so much," Pamela said sincerely. "You've been so supportive of me."

"This is a worthwhile cause. What you're doing is really beautiful."

"I'm not just referring to today. You are always supportive of me, Duncan. I want you to know how much I appreciate it."

"I know you do," Duncan said, pulling her close and kissing her sweetly.

"It goes both ways, you know," Pamela muttered as she snuggled into Duncan's chest. "If you ever need someone to lean on, I'll be there for you."

"I'm glad to hear that because I have something to tell you." Duncan took a deep breath and continued. "I'm going to Scotland for the last two weeks in August and I was hoping you'd come with me. I'll pay for the airplane tickets and I have family we can stay with. So, all you have to do is get your parent's permission and say yes."

With wide eyes, Pamela looked up at Duncan and asked, "Are you serious?"

Smiling, Duncan nodded.

"Yes! Of course I'll come!" Excited, Pamela squealed and hugged Duncan tightly.

Duncan laughed before saying, "We can go over all the details later. Right now you have a mission to complete."

Pamela walked Duncan to the door, all the while thinking about her upcoming trip.

Duncan had left just minutes ago when the doorbell rang.

"Hi," Lila greeted when Pamela opened the door.

"Hey, Lila! Come in."

"Thanks. I'm so glad for this break. I totally need it. Don't you feel the same?" Lila noticed Pamela looking out the living room window. "Is everything okay? You seem a bit distracted."

Pamela continued to stare silently out the window.

"Pamela! Are you even listening to me?"

Pamela didn't have a chance to respond as the doorbell rang.

"Did you invite Duncan over?" Lila inquired.

"No," Pamela said, remaining stationary.

"Are you going to answer the door?" Lila asked with rising suspicion.

"Yes, but I think I should tell you something first. Jeannie's the one behind the door."

"What?"

"Calm down, Lila. I'm just trying to fix things."

"That's commendable but you should've told me what your plans were," Lila said as the doorbell rang again. "You've really caught me off-guard."

"I'm sorry, but you wouldn't have come if I said Jeannie was coming as well."

"That's not true. I would've come. I miss Jeannie so much," Lila confessed as she approached the door and then opened it.

"Lila!" Jeannie exclaimed upon seeing her estranged friend.

"Hi, Jeannie," Lila said shyly.

"What are you doing here?" Jeannie asked, more curious than angry.

"Pamela invited me over."

"Pamela invited *me* over," Jeannie argued.

"I invited you both," Pamela said.

Lila and Jeannie turned around to look at Pamela.

"I was hoping that you two would make up upon seeing each other," Pamela explained.

"You didn't have to trick me," Jeannie said as she stepped into the house.

"Would you have come?" Pamela pried.

Jeannie avoided the question for a few moments by looking at the floor. "Yes," she finally said, looking up. "I've missed you, Lila."

"The feeling is mutual," Lila told Jeannie with tears in her eyes. "I regret all the cruel things I said about you."

"Don't say that," Jeannie said firmly.

"Why...why not?" Lila stammered.

"We needed to tell each other how we felt. We needed that time apart."

"Jeannie's right," Pamela spoke up. "I know that I didn't temporarily lose what you two did, but even I felt the consequences of your feud. However, it made me appreciate the great friendship that we all share."

"I feel the same," Jeannie said with tear-filled eyes as she embraced Pamela. She then turned to Lila. To her surprise, Lila hugged her.

"You're right," Lila stated. "I meant what I said while we were camping. However, I don't feel that way anymore. Michael isn't in my life. My father and I are saddened by what he did, but we've accepted it. The question is, have you?"

"Yes," Jeannie replied. "And in some ways, I'm thankful it happened."

"What?" Lila cried. "Why in the world would you say that?"

"If it wasn't for Michael's behavior, I would've never learned to appreciate the friendship which you, Pamela and I share. His actions also motivated me to work with the women's help center where I've really made a difference. It's ironic, but due to Michael, I've gained so much."

"And he's lost a lot," Lila added.

"I think we've all healed," Pamela stated before heading to her bedroom. "Follow me. I want to show you both something."

Jeannie and Lila cast each other curious glances but followed Pamela anyway. They stopped at the closed door and waited anxiously while Pamela opened it.

"Oh my gosh!" Lila said with a laugh as she saw the numerous photographs.

"This collage looks fabulous," Jeannie commented as she looked at it.

"I'm glad you guys like it," Pamela said happily. "Duncan helped me set it up."

"Where is Duncan?" Jeannie asked with a laugh as she studied a photograph of Pamela giving Lila bunny ears. "I've talked to him with Pamela on the phone, but I've never met him."

"You haven't?" Lila asked with wide eyes. "Then you're in for a treat – he's absolutely gorgeous!"

"Hey! That's my boyfriend you're talking about!"

"Look, Jeannie, there's a photograph of Pamela and Duncan in the collage."

Jeannie looked at the photograph which Lila was pointing to. "He *is* cute," she agreed. "I thought this collage was just about us though?"

"It…it is," Pamela stuttered, slightly taken aback.

"Relax, Pamela, I'm just joking," Jeannie said quickly. "I would be honored if Duncan joined our group."

"I'm glad you feel that way," Pamela replied. "Duncan's a big part of my life."

"Then I look forward to getting to know him," Jeannie concluded.

"So do I," Lila said. "Maybe he could even introduce Jeannie and me to a couple of his friends."

"I'll see what I can do," Pamela said with a laugh. She smiled widely as she watched Jeannie and Lila point to photographs and chat excitedly about them. It seemed as if they had a lot of catching up to do. Pamela was certain that she, Jeannie and Lila would make many more memories that they could one day reminisce about.

Although Jeannie, Lila and Pamela's friendship had been tested several times throughout the last year, they had met the challenges and were stronger than ever before.

* * *

About the Author

Heather Beck is a Canadian author and screenwriter who began writing professionally at the age of sixteen. Her first book was published when she was only nineteen years old. Since then she has written several well-reviewed books.

Heather recently received an Honors Bachelor of Arts from university where she specialized in English and studied an array of disciplines. Currently, she is working on two young adult novels and has five anthologies slated for publication. As a screenwriter, Heather has multiple television shows and movies in development. Her short films include *Young Eyes*, *The Rarity* and *Too Sensible For Love*.

Besides writing, Heather's greatest passion is the outdoors. She is an award-winning fisherwoman and a regular hiker. Her hobbies include swimming, playing badminton and volunteering with non-profit organizations.